Liron's Melody

Brieanna Robertson

Whimsical Publications, LLC

Florida

Liron's Melody is a work of fiction. Names, characters, and incidents are the products of the author's imagination and are either fictitious or are used fictitiously. Any resemblance to actual events or persons, living or dead, is entirely coincidental.

To purchase the authorized electronic edition of *Liron's Melody*, visit
www.whimsicalpublications.com

Cover art by Shyanne England
Editing by Janet Durbin

ISBN-13: 978-1-63495-024-4

Published by
Whimsical Publications, LLC
Florida

Before her parents' accident, the three of them had lived and breathed music. It had been the three of them for Melody's entire life. While she'd had friends and had never been a loner by any means, she had always preferred the company of her mother and father above everyone else. They all understood one another. They all spoke the same language—music. There was nothing now that they were gone. There had been nothing for the last year. No music. No joy. No nothing. So she filled her days up with mundane things that didn't matter, distractions, just to get by.

She had a job, a pitiful one, working as a sales clerk in a women's clothing store. She hated it with a passion. It wasn't her, but that was why she had taken it. It had nothing to do with music, nothing to do with the life that had been shattered.

But as she thought about it, she realized she wasn't really accomplishing anything by avoiding all that had once reminded her of what she'd loved. Like Rob had pointed out, she still had pictures everywhere of her parents and the orchestra they had all been a part of. And she couldn't escape the fact that the love of music still lived within her. It wasn't going to disappear just because she turned her head the other way and pretended she didn't see it.

She'd done everything in her power to alter her life to not revolve around music and the memories that would cause her pain, but it had only ended up causing her pain anyway. And it made her sick to her stomach to think that, by turning her back on what had made her life with her parents special, she had inadvertently turned her back on them.

Self-loathing washed over Melody in waves while Nikki's words from earlier repeated in her mind. She had been right about one thing. Her parents *wouldn't* have liked her current course of action. It would have saddened them to see Melody give up everything she had loved, everything she had worked for, just because she was hurting, just because she was afraid.

She heaved a sigh as she got out of the tub, pulled the plug, and dried off. She slipped into a light pink tank top and gray pajama bottoms and headed into the kitchen. She put on the teakettle, thinking a cup of tea sounded relaxing, and relaxation was the driving force of the evening, considering how rigorous the day had been.

As she wandered back into the living room, her gaze fell upon the score of music she'd set on her piano. She stared at it for a second, chewed on her bottom lip in contemplation, and then went over to give it a closer look. She picked it up and flipped through it gently, careful not to damage the well-worn pages. Glancing over the notes, she tried to imagine what it would sound like, but came up short. Nothing her mind could conjure would come anywhere near what it would actually sound like when played.

She set the music back on the piano and stared at it a few minutes more, curiosity gnawing at her. She was racked with indecision, not wanting and yet wanting to play it all at the same time.

She closed her eyes and took a deep breath, trying to force some calm to return. Okay, no one was there. She didn't need to worry about what anyone was going to say, and no one was going to make a big deal and throw a party and gush over how much progress she was making. And she wouldn't be playing "Adagio in G Minor," which was really what she had a problem with more than anything.

She'd play for a second, just to see what the score sounded like, and if she started to feel like her chest was going to constrict and she was going to have some kind of anxiety attack, she would stop. Simple as that.

Making up her mind, Melody tentatively slid onto the piano seat and poised her fingers over the keys. She let them rest there for a moment, testing the waters, so to speak. A twinging pain went through her heart and left a dull ache in its wake, but it was tolerable. Sucking in a breath, she looked at the first measure of music and began to play.

It was a mournful song, slow and dark, gothic almost. She had planned to stop after the first few measures, but once she started, two things happened. Wondrous ecstasy coursed throughout her entire body as the music filled her soul once again, and her fingers moved over the keys with grace and ease, like she had never stopped playing. For one beautiful second, she felt like she'd come home. That reason alone was enough to keep her there, but something else happened. Something strange and all-consuming.

Acknowledgements

This one is all for Travis Barton.

For acceptance, for listening,
for putting up with my eight billion text messages.
And for reminding me that all great artists are crazy.

You are a friend, and a man, without equal.

Also by
Brieanna Robertson

"A love song is just a caress set to music."
-Sigmund Romberg

Chapter One

"Geez Louise, this is the oldest piece of music I have ever seen in my life. Where did you get it?" Melody tentatively picked up the tattered, yellowed score her friend had put on her table, afraid it might fall apart in her hand.

"This big estate sale," Nikki said. "There was all this rich lady stuff there. Not really my style." She shrugged. "But I saw that thing and just had to get it for you. Can you still see it well enough to play it?"

Melody felt the color drain from her face, and she dipped her head, pretending to be engrossed in the ancient score. Really, she wanted her mass of blonde hair to fall in front of her face so Nikki wouldn't see how pale she knew she'd gotten. "The notes are still legible," she muttered, steering away from the actual *I can still play it* part of the statement.

She perused it a little longer, just to be safe, but when she stood straight and looked back at her friend, she knew she hadn't fooled anyone. Nikki had known her too long.

Nikki was staring at her, hands on her hips, her lips drawn into an unamused line. "Gimme a break, Mel. I wasn't born yesterday. You still haven't played anything, have you?"

Her face, which had felt so colorless a second ago, flooded with warmth, and she averted her gaze. "I may have played Chopsticks at one point."

Nikki snorted. "Awesome. A world famous concert pianist, trained at *Juilliard*, played Chopsticks once, probably when you were drunk. Alert the media."

Melody scowled at her. "Gimme a break, Nik. I wasn't world famous by any means."

"You could have been! Would have been if you had kept going!" She huffed out a sigh, and her expression changed from annoyed to sympathetic. "Melody, how long are you going to do this to yourself? They wouldn't have liked this.

Music was their life. Aren't you honoring their memory more by continuing on with what you all loved doing together?"

Pain squeezed Melody's heart, and her eyes burned, but she knew tears would never actually manifest. She hadn't cried since the accident. Not even at the funeral. "I can't, Nikki," she admitted softly. "I've tried, believe me. I just can't. Every time I sit down at that piano, all I see is the day before it happened. I see my dad busting one of his cello strings because he'd been playing like a maniac. And then Mom broke into an impromptu performance of Albinoni's "Adagio in G Minor" while he replaced it, which I accompanied her with on the piano. You know they played that song at their funeral, right? That was the last thing I played. I sat there and played that mournful, awful, exquisitely beautiful song with my mother the day before she died. And afterward, my dad said, 'There is no symphony in this world that matches the beauty of my two girls.'"

Melody shook her head as the pain around her heart became excruciating. "I played that with them and then they played it at the funeral. I didn't even know anyone had planned it. It had all been without my knowledge. The entire flipping orchestra played it because it had been their favorite piece of music. I can never listen to that again without seeing that day. And every time I look at my piano, that's what I remember."

"But the memory you have is a good one, Mel. Of the three of you."

"The memories are linked now. I see Mom and me playing, and then I see the funeral. I relive it every time I look at the piano. And, I mean, honestly." She huffed and held her arms out helplessly. "How can I play with them gone, Nikki? All of this doesn't mean squat without them."

Nikki's brown eyes filled with the tears Melody couldn't shed, and she sighed. "But, Melody, this was your dream, too. Not just your parents'."

"It was our dream together, and it died in that car crash along with them. I hear nothing now. No notes. No chords. I feel nothing. It's all hollow now. Why should I play when I feel nothing but emptiness?" She thumbed the frayed edges of the music score Nikki had brought her, desperate to be away from this conversation and this subject.

Nikki worried her bottom lip between her teeth, obviously fighting over whether or not to say something else.

Melody huffed. "Spit it out, Nik."

"You were working on that composition before—"

"Concerto," she corrected. "I wasn't writing a thesis, I was writing a concerto. And that was written with the purpose of featuring me, Mom, and Dad. I'm not going to keep writing it when they aren't here, no matter how much the orchestra members and the conductor, and the freaking ticket salesmen and janitors keep harping on me."

Nikki held her hands up in a sign of surrender as Melody's voice rose in pitch and vehemence. "Okay, okay! I wasn't trying to bug you, I was just saying, is all." She blew out a breath that sent the tendrils of brown hair around her face flying. "At any rate, I bought that thing for you because I thought you would like it. Play it, don't play it, hang it on your wall, use it for toilet paper. I don't care."

The irritation deflated out of Melody and was quickly replaced by guilt. She glanced down at the score again and sighed. "I'm sorry, Nikki. I didn't mean to snap at you. I do like it. It's beautiful." She picked it up and leafed through the fragile pages. For some reason, the worn paper reminded her of herself. They were tattered and lonely, brittle and stained, just like she was. Suddenly, the gift meant the world to her, and she clutched it to her chest. "Really, I'm sorry." She met her friend's eyes and shook her head. "I know you were only trying to help."

Nikki waved her hand. "Don't worry about it, Mel. I need to learn how to mind my own business." She gave her a gentle smile then raised an eyebrow playfully. "On a completely unrelated subject, have you seen Rob lately?"

She rolled her eyes and, with great care, set the music score on her piano. Maybe she wouldn't play it, but it looked wonderful there. If it was as old as it appeared, it deserved to sit in a place of honor. "He came by yesterday, bothered me until I went to dinner with him."

"How did that go?" Nikki giggled.

Melody shrugged. "All right, I guess." She turned away from her piano and met her friend's gaze. "I don't know. He's nice enough...most of the time."

"What do you mean most of the time?"

"Well, he's a little bit domineering for my taste. He orders for me. It's weird."

Nikki laughed softly. "Well, there are worse things."

"Yeah, I guess." Rob was actually her neighbor who lived across the street. He had moved in about a month ago and had been after Melody ever since. At first, she'd found it annoying. She wasn't really looking for a boyfriend. She was still having enough difficulty getting through the day and dealing with her grief over her parents. And they had absolutely nothing in common. He was a football coach at a local high school, and liked to watch Nascar and go to cage fighting competitions. He was bullheaded and wouldn't take no for an answer.

After a good two months of him not letting up, she had finally agreed to go on a date with the guy just to get him off her back. She'd been surprised that, though she had no interest in hunting, fishing, or dirt biking, and he had absolutely no care for any kind of music that wasn't screaming guitar, they did have a small measure of chemistry between them. He wasn't her type at all, but maybe that was why she kept giving him a chance. He had nothing to do with music, and therefore, nothing to do with anything that caused her pain.

"Speak of the devil," Nikki said, pointing her chin in the direction of Melody's front door.

She sighed as she turned and spotted Rob on her porch, peering inside the screen door to try and get a look at what was going on. "Hi, Rob," she called, unable to sound as enthusiastic as he probably wanted her to.

At the sound of her voice, he stood up straight and grinned. Dressed in denim shorts and hiking boots with a baseball hat and aviator glasses, he looked like everyone's All-American guy. "Hey, Mel, you busy?"

She went to the door with Nikki, who sent her a wink and said she would call her later. She moved past Rob and let herself out. Melody stood in the doorway, not allowing Rob to come in, just because she didn't want him to think he had a right. He was pushy, and she was tired of him trying to bully his way into her life. She enjoyed his company, was trying to let her guard down enough to see if they could actually have a relationship, but something about him still rubbed her the wrong way. "What's up?" she asked, folding her arms over her chest.

His grin never faltered. "I was wondering if you were do-ing anything today? I was thinking of going on a hike. It's a nice day, and I know a lot of good scenic trails. Thought maybe you'd like to come with me."

Melody mulled his offer over for a minute, then decided that it couldn't hurt. She wasn't much for hiking, but it would give her something to do. At least it was better than sitting at home with all the ghosts and the skeletons in her closet. "Yeah, okay. Just let me put on some decent shoes." She moved away from the doorframe and held the screen open for him, finally allowing him entrance.

Rob sauntered in and took inventory of her house like he hadn't already been there three times before. His eyes lin-gered on the pictures in the living room, which were all black and white photos of her parents and the orchestra. He frowned. "When are you gonna take these down?"

Melody arched an eyebrow at him. "I'm sorry, was I sup-posed to?" She couldn't have kept the sarcastic note out of her voice if she'd wanted to. She opened up the hall closet and grabbed a pair of hiking boots.

He looked at her and shrugged. "Well, it's just... I mean, isn't it kind of depressing to have those reminders every-where?"

"It was part of my life for a long time, Rob. And it's my house, not yours, so I don't need your approval." She sat down on the sofa to put her boots on.

He snorted. "Well, it isn't really your house, is it, Mel? It's still your parents'."

She frowned up at him. "No, it's mine. They left it to me in their will."

He rolled his eyes and indicated the pictures he had been talking about. "No, I mean it's still *theirs*. You haven't changed a thing, have you?"

Melody exhaled a measured breath. What was it with to-day? Everyone was a freaking therapist.

He must have picked up on her annoyance because he held his hands up the same way Nikki had. "Sorry, I'm not trying to stick my nose in." He met her gaze and his voice grew softer, if slightly patronizing. "All I'm saying is that they've been gone for a year now. You claim you don't want anything to do with playing music ever again, yet you still have all these reminders everywhere. I think it's unhealthy."

She finished lacing up her boots and stood abruptly. "Great. I don't remember asking you for your opinion, though."

He took a step back. "Geez. Testy. Fine, I'll put a lid on it."

"You do that. Otherwise, forget our date." He muttered something under his breath, but she couldn't hear what it was because she was on her way into the kitchen to grab a water bottle. Maybe she was being unnecessarily witchy, but she was really sick of people trying to tell her what was best for her. They weren't her. They weren't in her shoes. She didn't care how well-intentioned any of the unwanted advice was, it was still unwanted. And if she didn't keep Rob in his place, he would dominate the conversation and the entire day. If she gave him an inch, the guy took fifty miles.

"Where'd you get this ugly thing? Looks like someone put it through a blender."

She heaved an aggravated sigh as she came back into the living room and saw Rob studying the score Nikki had brought her. "Nikki got it for me. It's old. Don't touch it!"

He snapped back the hand that had been reaching for the music and stared at her like she'd lost her mind.

She scowled. For some reason, the thought of him touching that beautifully broken score made her extremely irate. She envisioned the already yellowed pages turning black and withering at the touch of his unappreciative hand. "Are we going or what?"

He moved away from the piano and gave her a measured look. He put his hands on his hips. "Did you want to take a Midol first?"

She opened her mouth to say something really rude, but before she could voice it, he chuckled and stepped forward.

He took her hands in his and shook her arms lightly. "Babe, what's wrong? Why are you so annoyed?"

"I'm just sick of people's opinions, Rob. First Nikki, and now you? Why don't we invite the mailman in and see what he has to say about my life while we're at it?" She tried to ignore the fact that he'd called her "babe." She hated that he tried to lay claim on her when they were not together.

Rob raised his eyebrows and moved his thumbs back and

forth across her hands. "I obviously didn't know Nikki had irritated you because I wasn't here. I'm sorry if I made it worse." He smiled, but she noticed it didn't really reach his eyes, which made her wonder if it was sincere at all. "If you don't want to go hiking, it's okay. I just thought maybe you'd like to enjoy this gorgeous day with me."

Melody sighed, feeling a little bit like a jerk. He really hadn't done anything to provoke her; nothing out of the ordinary anyway. He was always opinionated. She didn't know why she'd expect him to be any different. "No, I'll go. Sorry. I'm just on edge."

He trailed his finger along her jawline. "Don't worry about it, babe. I'll help you forget whatever's bothering you in no time."

She didn't say anything about his arrogant remark. Those also came with the territory when she was with Rob. She secured her hair back into a ponytail and followed him out the door. As she turned her key in the lock, a distant part of her mind screamed at her that she was insane, that this wasn't who she was. That nothing she had been doing for the last year of her life was productive or useful in any way. That all she was doing was hiding and running.

She hated that voice's opinion even more than she hated Nikki's and Rob's. So, she ignored it completely.

Chapter Two

Melody let the door crash closed behind her, not caring that it made a racket that probably could be heard all the way down the street. Her feet were screaming at her, she felt like her lungs were going to collapse, her quads felt like they were made of jelly, and her mood had not improved any. Apparently, Rob's idea of a "hike" was actually an Iron Man death march up the side of a mountain where he took off like an Olympian and left her behind, wheezing and puffing and almost falling to her death. And to make things even better, he had heckled her the entire time, calling her slow and out of shape.

The man had actually asked her if she wanted to eat dinner with him afterward. Even if she hadn't felt like throwing up from overexertion, she would have told him to cram it up his backside. He'd continued to tease her all the way home, thinking, she imagined, that he was funny. She wanted to kick him in the jewels. At times, Rob could be witty and charming. Those times were redeeming and were why she continued to keep him around. Other times, he was just a jackass.

After flopping down on her sofa, she yanked off her hiking boots and flung them across the room in frustration. She was finished with him for about a week. He could sit over there and figure out why she was annoyed. If he had a brain in his head at all, he wouldn't have a hard time with it. But then again, he was a guy, so who knew? Knowing him, he'd think she'd fallen madly in love with his primal, alpha behavior. In other words, the fact that he'd acted like a complete caveman.

She rolled her eyes and stood, heading down the hall. She pulled her clothing off and threw it haphazardly around her bedroom, grabbed her pajamas, and made her way into the bathroom. After she had drawn a steaming hot bath, she stepped into the tub and lay back in it with a sigh of bliss.

As the hot water relaxed her tired, tense muscles, she let her mind replay the day, specifically her outing with Rob. Sometimes she wondered why she continued to indulge him. He irritated her seventy-five percent of the time. Try as she might, she couldn't see herself falling for him. He was cocky and flip, and self-centered.

In the back of her mind, she knew the real reason she kept him around. It wasn't because she was interested in him. It was because he was a distraction. It kept her from thinking about anything in her life that reminded her of the past. Rob was about as far from what her life had been as she could get.

Before her parents' accident, the three of them had lived and breathed music. It had been the three of them for Melody's entire life. While she'd had friends and had never been a loner by any means, she had always preferred the company of her mother and father above everyone else. They all understood one another. They all spoke the same language— music. There was nothing now that they were gone. There had been nothing for the last year. No music. No joy. No nothing. So she filled her days up with mundane things that didn't matter, distractions, just to get by.

She had a job, a pitiful one, working as a sales clerk in a women's clothing store. She hated it with a passion. It wasn't her, but that was why she had taken it. It had nothing to do with music, nothing to do with the life that had been shattered.

But as she thought about it, she realized she wasn't really accomplishing anything by avoiding all that had once reminded her of what she'd loved. Like Rob had pointed out, she still had pictures everywhere of her parents and the orchestra they had all been a part of. And she couldn't escape the fact that the love of music still lived within her. It wasn't going to disappear just because she turned her head the other way and pretended she didn't see it.

She'd done everything in her power to alter her life to not revolve around music and the memories that would cause her pain, but it had only ended up causing her pain anyway. And it made her sick to her stomach to think that, by turning her back on what had made her life with her parents special, she had inadvertently turned her back on them.

Self-loathing washed over Melody in waves while Nikki's words from earlier repeated in her mind. She had been right about one thing. Her parents *wouldn't* have liked her current course of action. It would have saddened them to see Melody give up everything she had loved, everything she had worked for, just because she was hurting, just because she was afraid.

She heaved a sigh as she got out of the tub, pulled the plug, and dried off. She slipped into a light pink tank top and gray pajama bottoms and headed into the kitchen. She put on the teakettle, thinking a cup of tea sounded relaxing, and relaxation was the driving force of the evening, considering how rigorous the day had been.

As she wandered back into the living room, her gaze fell upon the score of music she'd set on her piano. She stared at it for a second, chewed on her bottom lip in contemplation, and then went over to give it a closer look. She picked it up and flipped through it gently, careful not to damage the well-worn pages. Glancing over the notes, she tried to imagine what it would sound like, but came up short. Nothing her mind could conjure would come anywhere near what it would actually sound like when played.

She set the music back on the piano and stared at it a few minutes more, curiosity gnawing at her. She was racked with indecision, not wanting and yet wanting to play it all at the same time.

She closed her eyes and took a deep breath, trying to force some calm to return. Okay, no one was there. She didn't need to worry about what anyone was going to say, and no one was going to make a big deal and throw a party and gush over how much progress she was making. And she wouldn't be playing "Adagio in G Minor," which was really what she had a problem with more than anything.

She'd play for a second, just to see what the score sounded like, and if she started to feel like her chest was going to constrict and she was going to have some kind of anxiety attack, she would stop. Simple as that.

Making up her mind, Melody tentatively slid onto the piano seat and poised her fingers over the keys. She let them rest there for a moment, testing the waters, so to speak. A twinging pain went through her heart and left a dull ache in its wake, but it was tolerable. Sucking in a breath, she looked at the first measure of music and began to play.

It was a mournful song, slow and dark, gothic almost. She had planned to stop after the first few measures, but once she started, two things happened. Wondrous ecstasy coursed throughout her entire body as the music filled her soul once again, and her fingers moved over the keys with grace and ease, like she had never stopped playing. For one beautiful second, she felt like she'd come home. That reason alone was enough to keep her there, but something else happened. Something strange and all-consuming.

While the sorrowful notes echoed through her empty house, her mind conjured up the image of a man sitting at a piano, alone in a candlelit room. She was looking at him from behind as he hunched over the keys, lost within the same notes she was currently playing. Long, shining, chestnut-colored hair spilled down his back and around broad shoulders that seemed burdened, as if they carried weight. That particular thing struck her because she noted that his shoulders looked the way hers felt. Heavy, tired, sad....

She focused on the image in her mind, more than happy to devote her attention to whatever her imagination conjured instead of the grief of missing her parents. The music filled her, swirled around her, along with the unbearable loneliness that emanated from the man at the piano. It was almost as tangible as hers, and her heart connected to him, whoever he was. An embodiment of her own pain and sadness, she imagined.

A chill ran the course of her body as the temperature in the room seemed to drop, which she thought was strange considering it was the middle of summer. She ignored it as she continued to play, driven by the gorgeous music and the enigmatic image in her mind. She found she wanted to know more about the person in her subconscious, the man brought to life by this aged score. It seemed he had a story to tell, and the only way to know it was to continue playing.

So she did. She gave herself over to the notes and chords, lost herself within the vision in her mind until it seemed almost real. The temperature in the room continued to cool and the hair on her arms bristled. She felt a strange tugging sensation around her heart, as if it wanted her to reach out to the man at the piano, touch him, soothe him, let him know he was not as alone as he felt, and maybe assure herself that she wasn't either.

As the music coursed through her and around her, she played with abandon. It was only when she shivered that she realized her eyes were closed, had been closed for quite a while. With a start, her fingers fumbled on the keys, causing the pristine notes she had been playing to falter. How could she be playing the music in front of her without looking at it? Had she just improvised the last few minutes? She stilled her fingers, but the melody of the music continued in her mind, echoing as if through a long tunnel. If she didn't know better, she would have thought it wasn't in her mind at all, but close by, and real.

Dampness touched her bare arms, and she swore she could smell the ocean, which made absolutely no sense considering she lived in Colorado, and nowhere near the sea. She looked toward her front door, wondering if she'd left it open and some kind of strange storm had rolled in.

She gasped and jumped so hard she almost fell straight off her piano bench. She squeezed her eyes shut and rubbed them with the heels of her palms. When she opened them again, everything was as it should have been, and the temperature in the room went back to normal. She stared at her empty living room, trying to figure out what she had seen. For a second, the half of the room she wasn't in had looked like some kind of stone structure, like a room in a castle. It had felt cold and foggy, dimly lit with flickering candles, and in the corner where the door should have been sat the man her imagination had conjured while playing the music. Only, she'd stopped playing, and he had continued.

"What in the world?" she whispered. Her heart pounded and her mouth felt dry. She glanced at the score of music and eyeballed it. She had never been an exceptionally creative person…not visually anyway, in the way of dreaming up strange visions. Even if she had daydreamed now and again, they had never been so vivid that they had taken up residence in the room she was in.

Maybe she'd finally lost her mind. Or maybe she was so exhausted from Rob's hike of death that her brain was playing tricks on her. That had to be it.

But even as she convinced herself that was the only logical explanation, her heart still ached at the sorrow she had felt while gazing upon that man. She glanced at the keys, part of her longing to play again, to see if she could glimpse him a second time. Part of her was afraid to. What if she really was losing her mind? Had grief and isolation finally caused her to crack? If so, it probably wasn't healthy to continue entertaining the fantasy.

But....

The desire to play again was overwhelming, no matter how irrational it was; no matter if he was a complete hallucination of her deluded mind. She just wanted to see him again. She wanted to see him because, in their shared sorrow, for one brief moment, she had not felt completely alone.

Exhaling slowly, she placed her shaking fingers back over the keys.

The shrill shriek of the teakettle made her nearly jump out of her skin, and she swore. She got off the bench, shaking her head and muttering to herself. It was probably a good thing the teakettle had whistled. She was literally one note away from the loony bin.

She went into the kitchen and turned the stove off, trying to put her mind to work on normal tasks. Hot water in the mug, tea bag in the hot water. She should probably eat something...she hadn't had dinner yet.

Play. Play.

Her subconscious was insistent tonight, probably because it wanted her to go crazy. She started to clean her kitchen counter while she waited for the tea to steep. *Scrub the counter, scrub the counter,* she chanted to herself. *Wipe it down, that's it. Nice and normal. Everyday tasks. Maybe I should clean the toilet next. I haven't cleaned the bathroom in over a week. It probably needs it.*

Play....

She left the sponge on the counter and turned to the fridge. She opened it up and perused the contents. It was pretty sad in there. She needed to go to the grocery store. Maybe she would do that next, after she had her tea.

Tea. She turned back to her teacup and bobbed the bag in it a few times. As she did, the image of that man flashed in her mind again. With the vision came the sorrow. His sorrow. His pain. It swamped her like a tidal wave until her chest ached.

She turned and leaned back against her counter. Was it possible for a figment of a person's imagination to be lonely? She had no idea. But, if he'd come from her imagination, she could understand why he would be. She couldn't remember what it was like not to be lonely.

Drumming her fingers anxiously across the tile of her counter, she sucked in a decided breath and strode purposefully back into the living room. She sat down at the piano and began to play again. Her curiosity was getting the better of her. She didn't care if she was losing it. She just wanted to see if he would come back.

The first few measures of the score tingled through her, and she felt the sadness in them in her body and soul. They took root in her heart, and she poured herself into playing the song. It was like someone had unknowingly written the theme of her life. The song sounded the way she felt...achingly alone, painfully isolated. And regardless of the beauty that still existed in the world, it was impossible to see any kind of sunrise within the all-encompassing darkness.

Tears burned her eyes, tears that wouldn't fall, and a chill went through her once again. She saw the man in her mind, but it was more difficult to concentrate on him when she was experiencing such turmoil within her own heart. She squeezed her eyes shut, dimly aware that she was still playing the song, and she focused all of her attention on the man at the piano. She didn't want to think about her pain, her loss. She desperately wanted to concentrate on anything else.

He became clearer to her, and felt closer the harder she thought. She heard the echo of the music as he played in his dismal room. The candlelight reflected off of his dark hair, making it shine and seem bronzed. Dampness touched her skin, and she smelled saltwater in the air.

She wanted to be closer. She wanted to see his face. She wanted to see if his eyes held the same hollowness she saw in her own when she looked in the mirror.

A loud knock on her door made her jump—again—and the vision vanished. She expelled a forceful breath, trying to get her heart to calm down since it felt like it was going to beat straight out of her chest, and went to the door. She yanked it open impatiently to see Rob standing there with his car salesman grin and a bottle of wine. Immediately, she wanted to sock him in the eye.

"What do you want?" she snapped.

He raised an eyebrow and his smile faltered, but only for a second. He held up the bottle of wine. "I know you said you didn't want to have dinner, and I got the distinct feeling that you were kind of aggravated at me earlier for leaving you to eat my dust on the hike."

He chuckled, and she found it to be the most annoying sound in the world. She folded her arms and leaned against her doorframe, blocking him so he couldn't try to push his way in, and she gave him a measured stare.

"I thought the wine could be a peace offering." He tried to peer over her shoulder into the room. "Hey, were you playing the piano?"

"Yes, I was." She snatched the wine from him.

"I didn't think you played anymore. Not since—"

"I didn't. But I decided I wanted to. Was this all?" She indicated the wine.

His smile disappeared. "Well, I was hoping that you would have a glass *with* me."

"I'm tired," she stated. "You tried to kill me today. I'm not in the mood to entertain guests. Thank you, though. The wine was thoughtful, and I'm sure I'll enjoy it. Goodnight, Rob."

He tried to protest, but she was not having any of his brashness tonight. She'd had enough of him earlier to last her for a month of Sundays. She closed the door on him and locked it, then took the wine back into the kitchen, where she set it on her counter.

Melody stared at her cup of tea, then poured it down the drain. She suddenly didn't want it. And she really didn't want dinner either. She felt exhausted.

Deciding she was done for the day, she headed toward her bedroom. She cast a glance back at her piano as she passed, but for the moment, the curiosity about what she saw when she played was gone. All she felt was the stark emptiness of her lonely house and her hollow heart.

Chapter Three

"She's gonna be a snob. I can assure you of that," Nikki said as they both got out of her sedan outside of one of the biggest houses Melody had ever seen in her life. "When I saw her the other day, she looked like a real Paris Hilton wanna-be."

"So long as she can tell me where that music came from, I don't care," Melody said, pushing a wayward strand of hair behind her ear. "That's all I want to know, and I won't bother her any further after that."

Nikki slid her a sidelong glance. "So, you really played it, huh?"

Melody met her gaze and sighed. "Yes, Nikki, I played it. Obviously."

"And how did your date with Rob go?" she asked with a smirk.

Melody rolled her eyes. "Please, I don't even want to go there. I don't know why I bother with that guy."

Nikki giggled and started toward the house. "He's proba-bly trying to impress you by acting all manly."

Melody snorted. "Well he can take his 'manly' and stick it where the sun doesn't shine."

Nikki laughed heartily. "You're feisty today!" she teased. "What got into you? You should play strange gothic piano music more often!"

Melody smiled in spite of herself. "It really was a beautiful piece of music. It touched me."

"Obviously, or you wouldn't be making me track down the lady I bought it from so you can ask about who the com-poser was." She fell silent for a few seconds, but Melody knew she wouldn't be able to hold her curiosity in for long. "So...how was it?"

"Playing?" Melody smiled. "It was heaven." She wasn't going to lie. Despite the pain of missing her family, playing the piano the night before had been like coming home from a battle. Music had always been the only thing to soothe her soul. It would always speak to her, regardless of whether or not she tried to avoid it. She knew, sooner or later, its pull would bring her back to it. It was unavoidable. And part of her felt at peace knowing that she'd finally crossed that barrier.

Her parents would have wanted her to keep playing. She knew that. They would have told her that music was therapy, and she should express all of her emotions, even the negative ones, through song. Surprisingly, the unbearable pain she had expected to feel while playing had never come. She had actually felt closer to the memory of her parents, and she knew she would not have trouble sitting down and playing again.

So long as she stayed away from "Adagio in G Minor." She wouldn't go near that piece of music with a ten-foot pole.

But she was interested in finding out more about the score Nikki had bought her. She wanted to learn about the composer, find out where the incredible music had come from. She was hopelessly intrigued, if a little creeped out, by the visions she had seen the night before. Her curiosity had always been more prevalent than her common sense. She had yet to figure out if that was a good thing.

Nikki rang the doorbell and they waited a few seconds until a very thin, blonde woman came to the door in an electric pink tracksuit chomping gum like a cow in a field chewing its cud. She had enough gold and diamond jewelry on to blind somebody, and Melody was shocked to see that she looked no more than nineteen or twenty years old.

"Hi," Nikki greeted. "You don't know me, but I was at your estate sale the other day. I bought this musical score. It was really old and worn-looking. Do you know what I'm talking about?"

The woman stared at Nikki for a second, blew a bubble with her gum, snapped it, and then sucked the gum back into her mouth in a completely classless gesture. "Yeah, I think I know what you're talking about. What about it? I'm not gonna give you a refund."

Nikki frowned. "Um...I don't want a refund. I was just wondering if you could tell me a little bit more about it."

"Like?" She sounded annoyed and glanced at her watch full of bling.

"Like who the composer was," Melody interjected.

The girl glanced up at her. "All those old music sheets belonged to my great-grandma. There was a bunch of crap up in the attic from, like, a hundred years ago. Took me freaking forever to go through it. My grandma kept everything. It was ridiculous. Took me *ages* to get this place looking like a normal house and not some kind of relic."

"Oh, this was your grandma's house?" Nikki asked, no doubt trying to be friendly and make conversation.

The girl snapped her gum again. "Originally, it was my great-grandma's. That's why all of her crap was in the attic. My grandma just died and left the house to me." She rolled her eyes. "Piece of junk. It's more trouble than it's worth, really. I'm thinking of just selling it once I get everything modernized."

Melody's stomach turned at the woman's cavalier, insensitive attitude. "Well, do you happen to know of any of the composers your great-grandma liked?"

She made a face. "How would I know? I don't listen to that crap. I listen to The Black Eyed Peas and Usher. You know, *real* music?"

Melody felt her eye twitch. Further proof that she was probably going crazy.

The girl waved her hand. "But all that crap in that trunk was stuff my great-grandma wrote. She was, like, this world famous classical musician. So that thing was probably her music."

Melody blinked. *Her* music. Somehow, that didn't seem right to her. She didn't know why. It made absolutely no sense, but that piece of music did not feel like it had been written by a woman. *No, of course not. It feels like it was written by some isolated man in a tower. What is wrong with you, Melody? You need a shrink, and pronto.*

Melody sighed and banished her wandering thoughts. "What was your great-grandmother's name, if I can ask?"

"Elizabeth Channing." The girl glanced at her watch again. "Is that all? I have a tennis lesson in ten minutes."

"Yeah...that's all. Thank you." Melody barely had a chance to get the words out before the girl shut the door on them.

Nikki snorted. "Nice." She turned and met Melody's gaze. "I hope you weren't looking for anything other than that."

Melody waved her hand and turned away from the door. "Nah. I know her name. I can look up the other information on the Internet."

Nikki gave her a curious expression. "You really want to know about the composer. That music must have been special to make you obsess that way when you haven't even wanted to look at music in over a year."

The image of the lonely, dark-haired man flashed through her mind, and her heart skipped a beat. *You have no idea.* She gave Nikki a smile she hoped was convincing. She had no intention of telling her friend that the reason she wanted to know about the composer was so she could see if she could find some reason for the strange vision she'd had. Some reason that didn't involve her checking herself into a mental hospital.

♦ ♦ ♦ ♦ ♦ ♦ ♦

Elizabeth Channing had been a gorgeous woman with pale skin, jet black hair, and smoldering dark eyes that looked like they could burn a hole through a person. And while her great-granddaughter had been right about her being a classical musician, she had failed to mention that she had only ever written the one piece of music—the nameless one that Melody held in her possession, which was probably worth a small fortune considering it looked like she had the original.

According to the trusty old Wikipedia, Elizabeth Channing, formerly Elizabeth Tabor, had actually been a classical singer and lyricist. Her husband, Aaron Channing, had been a composer, and had collaborated with her on a number of pieces that were still widely recognized and renowned, especially abroad.

Melody was baffled that, after all of her training, and with all the knowledge both of her parents had, she had no clue who either one of them were. And there was absolutely nothing she could find online that linked Elizabeth to any man other than her husband. And he was definitely not the man Melody had seen in her mind. Not that she really would have felt better if he had been. She didn't know which discovery would be worse—finding out that she was going crazy, or finding out that she suddenly had some sort of psychic ability.

After exhausting her search, Melody left her computer, no more enlightened as to what she had seen the night before than she had been when she started.

She made herself some pasta with meat sauce and garlic bread, having gone to the grocery store after her outing with Nikki, and opened up the bottle of wine Rob had brought over the night before.

As if the man had freaking radar, he knocked on her door as soon as she had finished pouring her first glass. Melody knew it was him without looking. He was relentless.

Melody went to the screen door and did her best to smile at him, even though she still kind of wanted to claw his face off.

"Hey, Mel," he greeted. "Whatcha up to tonight?"

"I just finished dinner, actually," she said.

He pouted in a way she imagined he thought would be cute. "Aw, that's too bad. I thought maybe we could grab a bite."

She shrugged helplessly. "Sorry, it's already made and dished up. Can't let it go to waste now."

"Well, do you have enough for two?"

She sighed. Talk about presumptuous. The guy had no limits to his pushiness. "Actually, thanks for the offer to hang out, but I think I'm going to take tonight and relax. I kind of want to play piano for a bit."

A strange expression crossed his face. "Oh, well...that's good, I guess." He scratched at the back of his head. "I thought you were done with that stuff."

She arched an eyebrow. "I don't think I was ever *done* with it. I just needed time to get over the memories it brought up."

"Oh...are you going to go back to playing in the orchestra?"

She frowned. Why did he sound so weird? What did it matter to him? "I don't know. I haven't thought that far yet. I'm just taking things one day at a time and enjoying the fact that I *can* play now. The orchestra is really the furthest thing from my mind at the moment."

For some reason, that seemed to make him relieved.

"Oh, all right. Well, have a good night then, Melody. You know where I am if you want me."

She ignored the implication behind his words and forced another smile. "Thanks. Goodnight." She closed the inner door and rolled her eyes, then went back to her now luke-warm dinner.

The food was mediocre. She had never been the best cook. The wine was rather exceptional, however. At least Rob had managed to get that right. She was about to pour her third drink when she decided to abandon the glass and go for the bottle. Who cared? She was a big girl. If she want-ed to drink an entire bottle of wine all by her lonesome, it was her own business. Even her parents wouldn't have stopped her if they'd been alive. They probably would have been there drinking right along with her.

She smiled at the thought of them, painful as it was, and migrated to the living room with her bottle. She stood in the doorway for a few seconds, staring at her piano. Taking a long drink of wine, she slid onto the bench, letting her eyes scan over the enigmatic piece of music on the stand.

Her mind was already hazy from drinking. She didn't drink often, so it didn't take much. Her usual anxiety about playing was diminished, an effect from playing the night be-fore coupled with the alcohol. The man she had seen still tugged at her heart in a way she could never explain or un-derstand. But she wondered if it really mattered. She had been filling her life with distractions for the past year. Maybe this was just another one. At this point, who cared? She couldn't deny that she'd rather distract herself with mystical men who appeared when she played music than with Rob, who appeared when he wanted to try and get into her pants.

She took another drink of wine and then set the bottle on the piano. She poised her fingers over the keys, drew in a soft breath, and began to play the haunting melody once again.

It didn't take long for it to enrapture her, to consume her, probably because the Cabernet she was drinking had lowered the barriers of her skeptical mind. She saw him again, alone at his own piano, and the volume of his sorrow was so stag-gering it almost made her fumble her playing. Each haunting note ached. Each measure bled loneliness. It echoed the pain within her own heart so perfectly that the line between his sadness and hers blurred, and she could no longer tell them apart.

Her eyes drifted closed as the music swept her away with its dreary beauty and perfect melancholy. The temperature in the room plummeted, and the hair prickled along her arms, the same as it had done the night before, only much more profound. She did not open her eyes to look around...she played on, wanting to make it through the piece. She wanted to know how the story ended, though she really wasn't sure what the story was. She just knew there was one. And she wanted to figure it out.

Dampness touched her skin and she heard the distant crash of ocean waves as she neared the end of the piece, the piece she had played three-fourths of by feeling alone and not by reading the music. Slowly, she opened her eyes while her fingers danced across the last few measures.

She sucked her breath in sharply, and her hands stilled. As before, half of her living room looked the way it had in her vision, only this time, it was so much more. The music continued, played by the solitary, dark figure over by where the door should have been. Her hardwood floors and white modern walls gradually turned into gray stone, and her electric lighting fizzled out into soft candlelight.

There was a surreal, dreamlike quality to the vision and she blinked hard, then glanced at her bottle of wine, wondering if maybe she shouldn't have drank so much after all. She picked it up and stared at it, then raised the bottle to her lips and took another rather lengthy drink. She half-expected the images to be gone once she lowered the bottle, but they weren't. The misty vision remained and she found her gaze drawn back to the man at the far end of the room, playing the music with no name that portrayed so perfectly the emptiness in her soul.

Entranced, she stood and took a few tentative steps forward, still holding her bottle of wine. Maybe she was drunk. Maybe she had fallen asleep at the piano and was actually dreaming. Either way, it didn't matter. She had to see his face. And she couldn't stand his painful isolation one more second. It was hurting her.

The sound of the notes became more resonant the closer she got, and the dampness she felt in the air intensified, as did the sound of the ocean waves. The room grew darker, and the highlights cast by the candlelight became brighter and more pronounced.

She stood behind him, watching the firelight play across his dark hair, watching his long, skilled fingers pull perfection from the keys. The haziness surrounding the vision began to dissipate, and the muted lines became clearer. Every note he played reverberated through her soul.

Slowly, she reached her hand out, moved by the beauty of the music and the fantasy she had fallen prey to. Her out-stretched fingers parted moist darkness until they caressed the length of his shining hair. The silken realness of it startled her, for she had honestly figured the entire dream would vanish upon her attempt to interact with it, and he did something she hadn't expected.

His hands crashed down onto the keys with a cacophonous sound, and he whipped around to look at her.

She jumped back with a little shout, stumbled over her own feet, and fell down hard on her backside, dropping the bottle of wine. It tipped over on its way down and dumped its contents all over the front of her. She gasped, and the shock of the liquid hitting her skin brought her rushing back to reality.

"Oh my goodness, are you hurt?"

Her gaze snapped to the owner of the voice—the tall, devastatingly handsome man looming over her—and she screamed. She scrambled into a standing position and turned, intent on running from this dream-gone-wrong and going straight to bed.

She screamed again. Her room was gone. Her house was gone. There was nothing familiar to her anywhere in sight. All she saw were stone walls, firelight, and when she whirled back around, the most beautiful man her eyes had ever had the privilege of looking at.

Her heart bludgeoned her rib cage with the force of its pounding, and her wine-fuzzy brain spun nauseatingly inside of her skull. She turned in a frantic circle, whimpering with bewildered terror. Upon seeing that nothing was going back to the way it should have been, no matter how hard she tried to search for her living room within the shadows of the dimly lit room, she decided it was a good time to scream again.

Chapter Four

"Oh man, oh man, oh man, I've really done it, haven't I?" Melody muttered to herself after she'd finished screaming. She tangled her fingers in her hair and squeezed her eyes shut. "I've really gone crazy. I'm hallucinating. This is bad. This is really, really bad."

"Madam?" The beautiful man stepped toward her with his hand outstretched.

Melody gave a shout and jumped back, stabbing her finger at him. "You stay away, hallucination!" She spun around again, searching for a way back to reality. "This isn't happening," she continued to mumble. "Come on, Mel. Wake up, wake up, wake up!" She smacked herself in the forehead repeatedly with her palm. When that didn't work, she closed her eyes and started to click her heels together. "There's no place like home, there's no place like home."

"Madam, please."

Melody's eyes snapped open to see him coming toward her again. She opened her mouth to scream again and had every intention of bolting, but he snatched hold of her wrist before she had a chance to do anything. His warm fingers encircled her arm and pulled her forward slightly while he trailed the fingers of his free hand down the inside of her forearm.

Melody's mind filled with the soothing sound of wind chimes and soft, tinkling bells. Tingles raced the length of her arm and calmed the frantic racing of her heart, replacing it with the lovely music of nature. She could hear the wind in the reeds while it stirred the chimes and it made her think of summer. Some clarity chased out the all-consuming panic that had been building within her; she let out a shaky breath.

She turned her gaze up into the man's eyes, which were the most amazing shade of blue, not unlike the summer sky she would picture to go along with what she heard. She glanced down to where he still trailed his fingers in lazy circles over her wrist, then looked up at him again. "H-How did you do that?" she whispered.

The smallest of smiles lifted one corner of his perfect mouth and warmth filled his gaze. "A gift," he replied simply. "Now, please, how in the world did you get here?"

She raised her finger and pointed at him. "No way! I will ask the questions!"

He raised his eyebrows. "All right."

"You are a hallucination, aren't you? My grief has finally done me in, and someone is going to find me in my living room, talking to someone who isn't there. Right? Admit it!" She was practically shouting at him in her attempt to gain some sort of control over this bizarre situation.

He blinked in bewildered silence for a moment before he drew in a soft breath. "What kind of hallucination would I be if I told you I was a hallucination?"

She stared at him for a second, then frowned. "Good point." She noticed he had let go of her wrist, and some of her spastic anxiety was trying to return. She felt it boiling up her throat and burning her eyes with tears she would have given anything to shed. She shook her head. "What is this? Who are you? Where the hell am I? How did I get here?" She fired the questions at him frantically while looking around her in an attempt to gauge her strange surroundings.

He reached for her hand, splaying her fingers so he could trace the lines in her palm. That wonderful, whispering calm returned, carrying with it the sounds of rushing water and rustling leaves.

"First question, this is strange. I don't know anything beyond that. Second question, my name is Liron. Liron Tabor."

Her brows drew together in a quizzical frown. "T-Tabor?" she murmured. *Elizabeth Channing, formerly Elizabeth Tabor.*

He nodded, and never raised the tone of his voice from calm, gentle, and velvet soft. "Third question, you are in my home. As to how you got here...." He shook his head and looked genuinely puzzled. "I have absolutely no idea. I did not know it was possible for humans to come here. And I certainly never expected one to sneak up behind me while I was playing the piano."

She blinked. "Human? You mean, you're *not* human?" She swallowed hard. "What are you?"

"A muse." His reply was simple, like she should have known what that meant.

"Muse?" she breathed.

He nodded and his gaze took in her features for a moment before his expression turned confused. "Do you have any idea at all how you ended up here?"

"I-I-My friend bought me this piece of music at a yard sale. I played it. It was beautiful. And when I played, I saw you. You were playing the same piece." His expression went from befuddled to kind of ill-looking. "Um...my living room...it changed. I could see you, playing. I could feel...pain, sadness." She frowned as all the color seemed to drain from his face.

"This music...who was its composer?" he whispered so quietly she barely heard.

"Elizabeth Channing," she murmured.

"Channing."

He averted his gaze to the floor and a wave of sorrow came off him so strong she felt nauseous. His fingers had tightened around her wrist to the point of pain, and she tried to shake her hand to get his attention. "Um...ow."

He snapped his focus back to her and immediately loosened his hold on her. "Oh!" he exclaimed softly. He feathered his thumb back and forth over her wrist and shook his head. "Forgive me for that." He slowly raised her wrist and placed his lips gently over her pulse.

Melody sucked in a breath and closed her eyes as she heard the crash of the ocean, night birds' mournful calls, all the sounds of the night, mystical and enchanting. Delicious shivers worked along her spine, and when he released her arm and she opened her eyes, something inside of her knew. As horrifying as the realization was, she just knew.

She stared up at him, into his azure eyes, and found the reality of her situation there. He gazed at her with kindness, with sympathy, with understanding that unsettled her. She shuddered, suddenly feeling very cold, and tears pooled in her eyes but refused to fall. "This...isn't a hallucination, is it?" she whispered.

He shook his head slowly, tender compassion turning his

eyes a darker shade.

"You're...really real, aren't you?"

He nodded, and she bit her bottom lip, feeling lost and terrified, like a little child who had been separated from her parents. And the truth was, that was exactly what had happened, and exactly how she had felt ever since that police officer had come knocking at her door a year ago.

"Wh-What are you?" she asked again, sounding about as small and helpless as she felt. "How did I get here? I want to go home."

He sighed and reached out to run his hands lightly down her bare arms. "Yes, I imagine that you do. Maybe we can figure this out if we sit down and talk. But before that, can you tell me what your name is?"

Her bottom lip quivered as she looked up at him. "M-Melody," she said, but it came out sounding more like a wheezing accordion.

His sinful lips turned up at the corners. "Melody...of course it is." His smile broadened, grew warmer, and she felt herself instinctively trusting him, which was not like her. But kindness radiated from every move of his elegant body. "All right, Melody. Could I interest you in a change of clothing? Something a little less...red?" He gave a soft laugh.

Melody glanced down at her wine-stained shirt and snorted. "Oh geez...I put on a white shirt. What was I thinking putting on a white shirt?" She looked like she had been stabbed repeatedly.

His chuckle was rich and lovely. "Well, I don't imagine you thought you were going to be traversing the continuum when you chose it."

That got her attention. "Continuum?" she cried, her voice going up in pitch. "Like, where Q lives?"

He frowned.

"*Star Trek?*"

The reference was apparently lost on him, if his perplexed look was any indication, so she shook her head. "You mean like the space-time continuum? Did I time travel?"

"Not exactly...."

"Not exactly? What do you mean not exactly?" She was vaguely aware of her voice getting louder again.

"There are dimensions that exist alongside, but are different from your reality," he tried to explain. To his credit, his voice remained amazingly calm, despite being thrown a strange woman who was on the verge of a psychotic break-down.

"You mean like a parallel universe?" She was almost shouting, and it was becoming increasingly difficult to take a decent breath. She felt like her airway was squeezing shut and that someone was standing on her chest. "What is this? I was never any good at physics! *I'm a musician!"* She wheezed in a much too shallow breath and held her arm out to him. "Could you? The wrist?" She shook it at him. "Because I think I'm go-ing to have the biggest panic attack ever if you don't."

He immediately took her hand gently in his and began to trail his fingers back and forth across her wrist. A small amount of calm returned to her, but it didn't chase all of the fear away. Her mind spun like a cracked-out roller coaster that had lost its brakes.

She ran her free hand through her hair and noticed how badly it was shaking. "Am I even on Earth anymore? Am I in outer space?"

He laughed softly. "You're not on another planet. You just managed to cross over into my world somehow, which I did not realize was a possibility until tonight. The music must have opened up a gateway of some kind, a bridge between the two of us." He shook his head. "I have known of muses who were able to travel into your reality, but I have never known of a human to come here."

"So what does that mean?" she all but yelled. "And what exactly is a muse anyway?" She sounded on the verge of hysteria. Actually, she *was* on the verge of hysteria. "This is so not what I had planned for tonight," she rambled. "I was going to drink, play some music that intrigued me, and let myself fantasize a little bit about some random guy I hap-pened to see when I played it. I did *not* expect to end up in some sub-genre of reality with—"

"Fantasize? About a man you saw when you played? If I'm following your story correctly, that man was me." He cocked an eyebrow in a playful, all too sexy gesture. "You were going to fantasize about me?"

Melody felt her cheeks flame, and that horrendous lost and isolated feeling came back with a vengeance. "That really wasn't what I meant." Her shoulders slumped, and she wanted to crawl into the nearest dark space and go to sleep, hoping that when she woke up, she would be out of this rabbit hole. "The wrist thing really isn't working this time," she said, hating how pitiful her voice sounded.

He let out a soft sigh and took her by the shoulders. "Melody, allow me to do something? It may help calm your nerves. But you need to stop thinking so much and listen to me."

She looked up into his eyes and studied the fantastic features of his face. Strong, chiseled, masculine features, yet with a subtle elegance that made him look ethereal and mythical...which she supposed made sense. What she loved the most was the benevolence radiating from his blue eyes. She detected no malice, no ill intent whatsoever. He was being infinitely patient and so careful not to frighten her more than she already was.

She forced a long, shaky exhale past her lips and nodded. "Please."

He stepped closer, slowly, deliberately, making no sudden movements that might startle her. He kept his eyes on hers, gauging her reaction while, with gentle certainty, he guided her into the circle of his arms.

Melody was startled at first, having not expected that, but as he pulled her to him and his arms closed around her, warmth unlike anything she had ever experienced enveloped her. This time, she did not hear the soothing sounds of nature. Instead, she heard beautiful, enchanting music. Soft, sonorous notes of such perfection that everyone in the orchestra she had once been in would have been envious. She heard instruments of all kinds—strings, wind, brass—all weaving a wondrous rhapsody that eased the frayed edges of her frazzled, overwrought nerves.

Her eyes slipped closed as she let the music fill her mind, and the strength of his body lent her the support she so desperately needed in that moment. She leaned into him without thinking, her cold, lonely heart starving for the warmth he offered.

"Shhh," he whispered as he smoothed his hand down the length of her hair. "I know you are frightened, and bewildered, but you are safe here. Nothing will harm you. I promise."

His voice made shivers dance throughout her, and his

constant touch and the contact of his body made the music in her mind continue, melting away all of her apprehension and terror. Tentatively, she wrapped her arms around his waist, surrendering to his embrace, and rested her cheek against his heart. The beat of it reminded her of a thunderous drum.

"I'm going to get your shirt all gross with wine," she said, because for some reason, that was very important to her at the moment.

His laughter was wonderful, and his arms tightened around her ever so slightly. "I don't care one bit about my shirt," he stated.

"I probably smell like a winery exploded." He, on the other hand, smelled like cedar and violin rosin. To anyone else, it might not have mattered at all, but to her, it was the world's most amazing smell. "Please, tell me what you are." At that moment, standing within his embrace as she was, with his caring reassurance and the music in her mind, she did not fear the answers quite as much.

"I told you. I am a muse." His words were hushed, his voice barely above a mumbled whisper, and he continued to drag his fingers through her hair in a calming gesture.

"But I don't know what that means."

"Muses inspire humans to create. There are many different kinds of muses. Muses who create stories, muses who inspire poetry, or lyrics, or art."

"And what kind are you?"

"I am a musical muse."

She smiled. "Well, that makes sense. Is that why I hear music when you touch me?"

"Yes. I control all elements of music. It exists within me. Even the music of nature itself. I can draw upon it and share it with you. That is how we help humans create."

"Did you know the woman who wrote that music I played?" She moved away enough to be able to look up at his face. "Did you inspire her to write that? Is that how it's all connected?"

A shadow passed over his features and his eyes grew sad. "She did not write that," he said.

Melody frowned. "She didn't?"

He shook his head. "No...I did."

She sucked in a surprised breath, but had a small moment of elation within herself. She had known when the girl from the sale had told her who the composer was that it hadn't felt right. And looking at the woman on the computer hadn't convinced her. When she'd played, when she'd heard Liron playing, the baleful notes had sounded like they were coming straight from his soul and were calling to hers. "But you know who she was?"

The light that had been in his eyes up to that point vanished and he looked away. "Yes. I did. She was my wife."

Melody's eyes widened. "Your wife?"

He nodded and met her gaze again. He gave her a smidgen of a smile, but she could tell even that much was forced. "If you think you are calm enough now, I will take you to where you can change into something dry. After that, we will have a conversation. All right?"

She agreed, feeling much more stabilized, if not any less confused. Her curiosity was beginning to take over where her panic had been, and now that she knew she was in this strange place, freaking out about it wasn't going to do her any good. It was disconcerting, sure, to suddenly find out that the world was not what she thought it was, but while she was stuck there, she may as well learn what she could about muses, and alternate realities, space travel...whatever it all was.

And especially about the handsome, sad man who filled her whole being with music.

Chapter Five

"You really do live in a castle?" Melody queried as he motioned for her to go first down the stone staircase that led to his bedroom.

He couldn't help but smile at her wide-eyed expression. The poor woman still looked utterly terrified. He couldn't blame her, really. This whole situation was completely strange, even for him, and he was very aware of alternate dimensions. "It's a little small to be a castle, but fashioned the same." He held his hand out, indicating that they were supposed to go down. "My bedroom is at the end of the staircase. I will give you a change of clothes."

She didn't seem the least bit interested in going down into the dimly lit passage, but she did so anyway. He allowed himself the pleasure of appraising her while they descended the staircase. She was very lovely, if slightly haphazard at the moment. Her hair was a beautiful honey-golden shade and it fell in wild waves around her shoulders, tangled from running her fingers through it so many times. She was wearing a snug, white sleeveless shirt and some gray pants that hugged the gentle curves of her slender body.

The way his body had instantly blazed to life with attraction for her the second he had seen her surprised him. He had been a cold, dormant chasm of nothingness for so long he'd figured Elizabeth had robbed him of any passion he'd once possessed. But something about Melody, complete stranger that she was, called out so strongly to him. Maybe it was the vulnerability he'd seen reflected in her pale blue eyes, the lost, terrified look that made him want to fold her up in his arms until she felt safe. Or maybe it was the fact that, despite being scared out of her mind, she had trusted him, leaned upon him, needed his protection and his care, regardless of the fact that he was something foreign to her, something odd and frightening. He didn't know if there had been a time in the past when someone had needed or wanted his protection. Elizabeth certainly never had.

He couldn't shake the memory of how Melody had felt in his arms, pressed against him with so much faith that he had not earned and did not rightly deserve. He'd been alone for so long, not creating, not inspiring, barely even existing. A human woman had somehow gotten a hold of his music, and for reasons he didn't quite understand, had managed to open a gateway into his world. And for other reasons he didn't understand, she had reached out to him. Whether she had believed she was dreaming or not, she had reached out to him all the same.

Melody swore suddenly as she stumbled on one of the stairs and caused a bit of a racket as she tried to catch herself. At the bottom of the staircase, there was some rustling before a large winged thing flew up the corridor. It narrowly missed Melody and she screamed, throwing her arms over her head and crashing into Liron's body as if he was her escape route.

His arms went around her, and he grunted as she knocked him back into the wall. He winced with the force of her banshee-like shriek, but warmth exploded along the surface of his skin where she was pressed.

She gasped and peeked out from under her arms. "Oh my gosh, was that a bat?" she murmured. "Like a real live *bat*?"

Liron grimaced as her voice started to take on that hysterical, shrill tone once again. "That was Siegfried," he answered.

She looked up at him, not moving out of his arms. "Siegfried?"

He nodded. "My falcon. He sleeps down here. We must have startled him."

"You have a pet falcon?"

He shrugged. "Not a pet so much as a companion."

She stared at him for several silent moments before she let out a shout laden with exasperation. "As if my nerves weren't shot enough!" she cried. "This night *sucks*!"

The corner of his mouth twitched. "Well, I can't say that I find it *completely* deplorable." He reached his hand up to smooth several out of control strands of her hair, tucking one of them behind her ear.

Melody met his gaze and drew in a soft breath. Color stained her cheeks as she grasped his meaning and she looked down shyly, but didn't move away from him. In fact, she seemed to curl into him even more, her soft body molding against his. If he had no other moments in his life, he would have gladly remained in that one forever, standing in his dreary hallway, holding her against him, basking in the warmth that surged through him at her nearness. It was the only warmth he had felt in so very long.

"Are there any other creatures I need to know about?" she asked. "Bats, birds? Vampires, werewolves, goblins, ghouls, ghosts?"

"No bats or birds," he replied. "And I made sure the vampires, werewolves, and all other paranormal creatures were safely locked in the dungeon, so they should be of no trouble to you." Her alarmed expression made him chuckle, which, in turn, caused her to break into a small, shy smile. He grinned and touched her cheek with his forefinger. "Ah, she smiles. Finally."

Her bashful smile grew broader, and she giggled a little.

Liron found the sound of her laughter to be the most beautiful sound he had ever heard. His gaze focused on her full, luscious lips, and he lightly ran his finger along the bottom one. "A woman with a mouth like yours should always smile."

Her cheeks reddened, and she dipped her head to avoid looking at him. She let out a long sigh and shook her head. "You must think I'm completely insane."

He frowned slightly. "Stop saying that. I have not once thought that."

She glanced back up at him, faint surprise mirrored in her eyes. "You haven't? But I invaded your house, from a different dimension no less. I screamed at you. I had a spaz attack, and then I screamed at you some more."

"Under the circumstances, I believe you had that right," he replied. He took in the delicate, soft planes of her face, the gentle curve of her throat and neck. "And, trust me, your presence here is anything but an invasion, Melody." Her gaze locked on his, her eyes full of wonder even though there were still traces of understandable apprehension. And beyond that, underneath the emotions brought about by the current situation, he detected a profound pain and loneliness not unlike his own. It tugged at the deepest roots of his heart, and he was swamped by the most overwhelming urge to hold her, protect her, show her the gentleness and compassion he himself had been denied for so long. It was wrong that someone else should have to endure the emptiness that he had. Especially someone as lovely as her.

Tearing his eyes away from hers, he forced his thoughts back to the task at hand. Staring at her like that would no doubt do nothing to make her feel any more at ease. "Shall we continue?" he queried. Then, unable to help himself, said, "Unless you want to stand here in the stairwell clutching onto me all night, which I admit, I am not completely opposed to."

"Oh." The word came out in a rushed breath, and she pushed away from him with another attractive blush.

He smiled and held his hand out to her. "Come. I will lead you."

She looked relieved and put her hand in his with no hesitation. He tried not to notice the warmth and softness of her fingers as he continued down the stairs and then the hall to his bedroom, but he lost that battle. He tried to remember if there had ever been a time when Elizabeth had held his hand, but he couldn't recall one. He'd never thought something so simple could be so wonderful.

He opened the door to his bedroom and pulled her inside. He lit several candles, as it was completely dark, and got a shirt out from his wardrobe. "I imagine this will be a bit large for you, but it's all I have," he said as he handed the clothing to her. "There hasn't been a woman here in a very long time."

Melody took the shirt from him and clutched it to her chest. "It's fine, thank you. I'm not picky."

He smiled and gave her a small nod. "I will leave you to change." He pivoted on his heel.

"Wait!"

Her cry stopped him in his tracks, and he turned back to face her. The concern on her face twisted his heart.

"Where are you going?"

"I'll be right outside the door," he assured her. "I will wait for you there. Then we'll go back upstairs and talk by the fire where it is warm and comfortable."

She seemed placated by that information and nodded. She looked down at the shirt she held and absently smoothed the fabric with her fingers. "Liron?"

He took a couple steps toward her, aching to hold her in his arms until she stopped looking so lost and frightened. "What is it, Melody?"

"Thank you for everything, for being so patient. My mind is still spinning. You have been so kind and understanding."

He smiled softly and reached for one of her hands. He bowed over it and kissed her fingertips. "It's my pleasure. Now, change your shirt. I'll be right outside." He strode from the room before he actually made good on his desire to take her in his arms. He was sure that would not put her at ease, even though it would be coming from a good place in his heart. She had trusted him so implicitly. He didn't want to do anything to jeopardize that. He wanted to talk with her, learn about her, find out what strange connection she had to him and his music. He didn't want to alarm her by being bold.

But as he closed his bedroom door and leaned back against the stone wall to wait, the memory of the two times she had been in his arms already plagued him. In less than an hour's time, she had thrown his entire existence off kilter. And he had to watch himself. She was a human, from the human world. He had no idea how she had ended up in his world, but she wanted to go home. And he couldn't blame her for that. But he would be a stupid idiot of a man if he allowed his attraction for her to root itself into his heart. Once she went back home, that would be the end of it.

He had no pieces of his heart left for anyone else to rip out. He had to guard what remained of it carefully.

Chapter Six

Melody smoothed her trembling fingers down the silky length of the black shirt after she had buttoned it up. It was long and slightly baggy, but not horribly oversized. Now that she was alone in the room, she took a moment to try to gather her wits so she wouldn't keep shouting at Liron like some kind of freak of nature.

She took a look around the room, which was cast in the sultry amber light of the candles. Whatever world she was in was messing with her brain. Liron lived in a castle with no electric light that she was aware of, but he wore modern-looking clothing. He had a pet falcon, and tapestries adorned his bedroom walls, but upon closer inspection of the room, she found a bathroom with a real toilet and a tub. It was like she'd gone back in time, but not. Weird.

She wandered around the room, trying to see if it gave away any clues about the man who lived there. The tapestries were the only real decorations, but he didn't need anything beyond them. They were beautiful and rich in color. One of them depicted several women dancing with flowers in their hair in lovely, flowing dresses. The other one was a menagerie of musical instruments amidst red rose petals.

His bed was colossal, something she would expect to see in a decorating magazine. It was a four-poster made of dark wood carved with intricate designs. As she studied them, she could see that even they were based on music. Clef symbols, measures, bars, and notes swirled around the spires as if music had been composed and written directly into the wood. She ran her fingers over it and sighed. So much for distracting herself with things that didn't have to do with music. She was surrounded by it, even had a man waiting outside who filled her head with it when he touched her.

That should have freaked her out, but it didn't. In fact, it did quite the opposite. Every time Liron touched her, she felt calmed, soothed, safe. It was completely bizarre. But even in the hallway after Siegfried had scared the ever-loving crap out of her and she'd crashed into Liron, she'd had no desire to move away from him. She had no idea what that meant. She wasn't sure if she cared at this point.

She left the bed and went to the window. It was stained glass, full of reds, blues, and greens. The design was nothing specific, just a beautiful pattern that added a finishing touch to an already beautiful room. A little bit gothic, a little bit medieval, but with indoor plumbing. She could work with that.

A soft knock on the door sounded and brought her out of her thoughts. She turned to look over her shoulder.

"Melody, are you all right?"

She smiled at his concern. The poor man probably thought she was in the corner sucking her thumb. "I'm fine," she called.

"Can I come in?"

"Yes, I'm changed."

The heavy door swung open and Liron entered. His eyes swept over her as if assessing her state of mind. "Something wrong?"

She shook her head. "No, I was just admiring your window."

He glanced at it and smiled. "Oh. It opens." He strode toward her and reached up to pull a latch at the top, then pushed the glass outward.

Melody was instantly blasted by fog and salty ocean air. The crashing of waves below drew her attention, and she peered down to see jagged cliffs and churning black water. "Oh my goodness," she breathed. "You have quite the view."

His smile grew and he leaned against the doorframe. "Nature's most powerful symphony. It's my lullaby."

She glanced up at him, captivated by his words. He closed his eyes and inhaled deeply as the sea breeze drifted over them and tossed a strand of his dark hair. The firelight from inside mixed with the silvery sheen of the full moon and played upon his face in the most amazing way, highlighting the prominent lines and shadowing contours. He was wickedly, brutally handsome, and when he turned his blue-eyed gaze to her, she lost her breath.

"Your music, that piece that brought me here some-how...." She shook her head. "It was so beautiful. I've never heard anything like it before. Not in all the classical pieces that I've played."

Darkness clouded his features and he averted his gaze. "I've never written anything since that." It was a soft admission, the words tinged with pain.

She stared at him, at the way the ocean breeze continued to tug at his hair, at the muscle that worked along his defined jaw, at the sorrow etched into his face. She wanted to touch him so badly, soothe him when she didn't even know what was causing the misery. "You haven't written anything?" she murmured.

He shook his head. "Hurt too much."

They were three words. Three very simple words that told her nothing and everything. It was a truth she understood all too well. It didn't matter that she still didn't quite know what he was or what was going on. It didn't matter that she was unaware of what had caused him such profound pain. The only thing that mattered was that, in the simple acknowledgement of deep heartbreak, they were the same. Through a piece of music he had written in his pain and she had played in hers. It made no sense at all that she could be transported to an alternate dimension and, yet, it made all the sense in the world.

She reached for his hand and gently took it between both of hers. She trailed her fingers across his wrist, then smiled up at him. "I don't imagine my touch has the same effect as yours."

A brilliant grin lit up his face, chasing away the sadness that had been there a moment before. He brought her fingers to his perfect mouth and pressed his lips to them. "Melody, there is no music I could ever compose that would express the effect of that one kind touch."

Melody's cheeks burned and she bit her bottom lip in a girlish gesture she hadn't done since high school. And if he continued to lavish kisses upon her hands the way he had been doing all night, she was going to lose her mind. They were so gentlemanly and chaste, yet they brought forth some kind of dormant inferno in her blood.

For a moment, the dismal look in his eyes was gone and

his smile was soft. "Come with me. We will sit and discuss things." He reached up to close the window and led her out of the room and back up the staircase.

Melody didn't find the passageway nearly as disconcerting as she had before and she found herself taking in more of her surroundings, exploring with curiosity instead of wanting to run and hide.

Liron's home, despite the gothic dreariness brought about by the candle and torchlight and the stone walls and floors, exuded warmth and classic elegance. It could have very easily felt like a dungeon, but it didn't. It felt more like she was walking in some kind of medieval work of art. Not surprisingly, it looked the way his music had sounded.

Once back in the main room, Liron indicated one of two large black leather chairs that sat on an intricate Persian rug in front of the fireplace. "Can I get you anything?" he asked. "Tea? Coffee? Another glass of wine?" A teasing smile lifted his lips. "A shot of whiskey?"

Melody laughed softly. "As tempting as that sounds, no thank you."

He sat down across from her, gazed into the fire for a moment, then sighed and leaned back in his chair. "My marriage to Elizabeth was an arranged marriage," he declared. "That is very common for muses. As a muse, our purpose is to connect with and inspire humans to create, to help make your world more beautiful. We can contact a human on a telepathic connection, usually in dreams. Our parents match us with a muse who will be a good complement. In my case, I was a musical muse, and Elizabeth was a lyrical muse. The idea is to match two muses of similar talents so that they will continue to inspire one another, thus being able to continue inspiring humans."

Melody listened intently, her mind spinning with this extraordinary new world she had never imagined could exist. She watched the firelight play across Liron's face, and noticed the sadness return as he spoke.

"I loved her instantly," he continued after a brief pause. His voice was raspy with emotion, whimsical, and tinged with disappointment. "The second I saw her, with her midnight hair and bottomless dark eyes, I was lost." He shook his head with a sigh. "She never shared the sentiment."

Melody frowned. "She didn't love you? I mean, she didn't grow to love you? After you got to know one another?"

He shifted his attention to meet her gaze for a moment, and Melody clamped her mouth shut. What was the matter with her? That was none of her business and definitely not her place to ask. She was curious and intrigued, but that didn't give her the right to pry into the man's personal life. She should be happy he was explaining anything to her at all.

"I'm sorry, Liron. That was rude of me. You don't have to answer that." She looked down at her lap and toyed with the hem of the shirt.

His baleful blue eyes stared at her for several moments before he reached a hand out to her. She scooted forward and slipped her fingers into his, relishing the way the gentle music filled her mind and soul.

"Melody, understand something. For whatever reason, my music provided a way for you to travel to this dimension. I didn't know that was possible. For it to have occurred even in a smaller measurement, we would have had to share a very strong connection. And not only that, but when the gateway opened for you, you had to have the courage to go through it, to reach out to me." He caressed the back of her hand with his thumb. "I have been isolated in this house for longer than I can remember. I don't know what made you step through that portal, but you did. You can ask me anything you desire."

He let go of her hand with a lingering touch and turned his attention back to the fire. "No, she never grew to love me. I did everything in my power to make her happy, but she never warmed toward me. She accepted me on our wedding night with a sort of grudging duty, I suppose, and after that, she slept in a different room. She would not come to me. Maybe I repulsed her. I don't know."

Melody snorted and he looked back over at her. She rolled her eyes. "Any woman who could find you repulsive is off her noggin," she grumbled.

Her comment made his beautiful smile chase away the shadows again, and he chuckled. "You are good for my self-esteem," he said. He paused for a second before he added in a low voice, "You'd better be careful. I might decide I want to keep you."

Heat flooded her body, and her heart skipped a beat. She didn't know which was more unnerving...his bold statement, or the fact that she didn't find it to be that unappealing of an option.

"Anyway," he continued. "To make a very long, boring, and painful story short, our marriage was a sad excuse for a relationship. It was six years of me aching for someone I could not have, who lived with me, ate with me, tormented me with her beauty every time she walked into a room. We both continued to inspire humans the way my kind have always done, the way we were taught. We existed together, but separately. And one day, she came to me and told me she was leaving. That she had fallen in love with the human man she was inspiring, a classical composer."

"Nice," Melody muttered. "I guess they were going to make beautiful music together." Her words were so sarcastic she could almost see them dripping acid. But she was rewarded with another chuckle from Liron, and it warmed her heart.

"You have a way with words, Melody, and a way of taking the dark stain out of this miserable part of my history. I thank you for that."

She smiled and continued to toy with the hem of his shirt, wondering why it was she could go out with Rob over a dozen times and have him fawn over her, but only feel annoyed, yet have Liron say one line of praise and feel flushed and bashful. Rob...he seemed like he existed a thousand miles away, like he was only a small part of a distant memory. At this point, her entire life seemed like a distant memory.

"Was the classical composer she was hot for named Aaron Channing?" Melody queried.

Liron raised an eyebrow and looked at her. "Yes."

She nodded. "When I went searching for who had written that music score, I did some research on Elizabeth and found out about him too." She frowned. "But when I was looking up the information, everything said that Elizabeth had written that piece of music, that it had been the only score she'd ever composed."

A different kind of shadow darkened his face. This one was not sadness, but anger. "When she told me she was leaving to go live in the human world, I begged her like a sad excuse for a man not to go. Living with her frigidness was better than not having her at all. She ignored me, as was her way. So, I wrote that piece of music. For her, so she would know how much sorrow and pain I felt, how much I still loved her. It was a gift and my last plea, the last amount of creative strength I had." He scowled fiercely and his voice took on a bitter bite. "She actually had the audacity to kiss me afterwards, the first amount of affection she had shown me since our wedding night. Told me it was the most amazing thing she had ever heard. Hope surged within me like a living thing, and I went to sleep that night feeling like maybe there was a chance for us after all.

"The next morning, she was gone, and so was my music. Her connection with her human was strong enough to enable her to travel to the human world. So, she'd vanished in the night like a petty thief, and had stolen the music I had written for her."

Melody gasped in outrage. "You mean she slapped her name on your music to make herself famous in my world?"

He snorted in disdain. "Apparently."

"What a bitch!" she spat. Liron looked at her with a surprised expression and she stood, stabbing her finger at him in agitation at the turn of events the story had taken. "She friggin' plagiarized you! If this had happened in my world, she could have been sued nine ways from Tuesday!"

Liron stood also and held his hands up. He smirked. "Melody, calm down."

"I will not calm down! That is absolute crap, Liron. What an awful woman. I'm glad I never knew about her and her stupid husband in all my studies. If I found out that I had once played one of his stupid scores, I would have wanted to vomit." She crossed her arms and tapped her foot in annoyance, angered that someone would intentionally hurt another person in such a calculated fashion.

"It happened a long time ago," he said.

"Yeah, and you haven't written anything since! She ripped your heart and your creativity out! She stole your music and your life!" Suddenly, his words hit her with a rush of realization. *It happened a long time ago.* That girl at the yard sale had said the music had belonged to her great-grandmother. Melody blinked rapidly. "Whoa, wait a second, how old are you anyway?"

He raised an eyebrow at her sudden change of topic.

"This Elizabeth cow has been dead for decades! Like, a whole lot of them!" She wasn't going to take the time to try and figure out exactly how many. That wasn't the point, and she didn't have enough fingers and toes anyway.

He smiled. "Time moves differently in the human world, faster. It was the one bit of satisfaction I was granted. To know that her time with the human was short, as opposed to how long of a life she could have had if she'd chosen me."

"So, are you immortal?"

He shook his head. "No, not by any means. But a year to a muse would probably be more like five for a human."

She stared at him. "Dang. That means you guys were actually married for...thirty-five human years?"

He dipped his head in a nod and stuck his hands in the pockets of his black slacks. "By estimate, yes."

"And she ditched you after all that time?" Her voice went up in pitch again. "What a whore!" His rich chuckle warmed her blood from head to toe in a way that was different from the anger surging through her veins. He stepped close to her and ran his hands gently down her shoulders, causing a thousand tingles to surge beneath her skin.

"Your vehement defense of me is very flattering," he said.

She snorted. "Well, I don't care which way you look at it, that situation is just jacked."

He didn't move away from her and exhaled a soft breath. "It's strange," he said. "But I have carried such bitterness within me from all of that. For all these years, I have festered alone with it, along with my sorrow, my loneliness. But look what happened. Because she stole my music, it found its way to you. And you, in turn, found your way to me. I know it has been harrowing, but do you regret the experience? Because I certainly do not regret meeting you this night."

Melody looked up into his eyes and found herself moving closer to him before she even realized she was doing it. "It's definitely a once in a lifetime kind of adventure," she said with a smile. Her heart started to thunder as he continued to gaze down at her, and she reached out to place her palms tentatively against his chest. He felt solid and strong, like the tower of refuge he had been for her during this entire bizarre event.

"It was your sorrow that called to me," she admitted quietly. "The loneliness you speak of living with for all this time. I heard it when I played that piece of music. I felt your pain because it was so similar to my own. That music called to me, lived within me. I could feel you...." She ran her hands down his torso slowly and shook her head. "Does that make sense?" She looked back up into his eyes, acutely aware of how close he was to her. She felt the warmth from his body, and she ached to be enfolded in that comforting musical embrace once again.

"None of this, in all reality, makes any kind of sense," he replied, his voice deep and hushed. "But what you speak of I, too, feel in a smaller measurement every time I look into your eyes."

Her gaze traveled to his mouth and her heartbeat accelerated. She wondered, if the man's lightest touch was full of the most amazing music, what would a kiss feel like? Was it bad to kiss a muse? A creature that, until several hours ago, she had not known to exist? Was it bad to be so forward with a stranger regardless of how incredibly sexy he was?

As if in answer to her, Liron's arms slipped around her waist, pulling her closer against his chest. Lovely sounds filled her mind. They chased away all doubt, all sadness, all pain. There was nothing but music, and the sound of her pounding heart as it reacted to his nearness.

And then a blaring, obnoxious siren of sound that jarred her brain and broke the moment with a vengeance. Liron winced and shook his head. Melody blinked rapidly and stepped out of his embrace.

"What is that awful noise?" Liron muttered.

Melody gasped as she looked over his shoulder. "Oh my gosh!" she whispered. Half of his room had, once again, morphed back into the modern décor of her house.

Liron turned to see what she was looking at, but didn't react with as much surprise as she would have. "Is this your home?" he queried.

"Yes," she said, stepping forward. "This is what happened when I came here. Only I was there, and I was peering in on you." She pointed to where she could see her piano. She frowned as she noticed rays of light filtering in from the kitchen window. "Holy crap, what time is it? How long have I been here? That noise is my alarm clock." She turned to Liron. "What happened? How did the gateway open again?"

He stared into her living room for a moment before his shoulders slumped in an almost indiscernible measurement. But she noticed all the same. "Apparently, all you needed was something from your world, a reminder, to bring you back home."

Relief rushed over her in waves, knowing that she was not permanently stuck in some strange dimension, but hard on the heels of that relief was disappointment. If she went back through the gateway, would she ever be able to see Liron again? Or would that be the end of it? Like a strange and beautiful dream?

She turned to face him and saw the same disappointment reflected in his eyes. He smiled, but not for the first time tonight, it looked forced. He stuffed his hands back in his pockets. "Well, Melody, I must say, it has been an honor and a privilege."

She managed a smile that she imagined looked as pained as his did. "Liron, this entire night has been...extraordinary. Terrifying, but extraordinary."

He took her hand and traced along the lines of her palm the way he had done to calm her earlier. "For whatever reason this happened, I will always be grateful. You chased away the loneliness, even if for a night, and made me remember what it is like to hear music, what kind of power it can have. I think I had forgotten that in my misery." He met her gaze and shrugged one shoulder. "My only regret is that I did not have enough time to learn more about you."

She opened her mouth to speak, but he brought her hand to his lips and pressed a lingering kiss to her fingers. A heady rush of notes filled her to the point that it almost made her dizzy.

"Go on before it closes," he murmured.

He released her hand, and she took a step toward her room, but hesitated. She looked at him for a long moment, trying to fix him into her mind. "You promise me you were never just a hallucination?" she asked.

He grinned, a real one that lit up his otherwise somber

face. "What kind of hallucination would I be if I told you?"

She smiled. "I'll never forget you." Even as she said the words, her heart felt funny in her chest, achy and longing.

"And for that, my life no longer seems so dismal."

He bowed at the waist, and Melody turned to hurry into her living room before she lost her nerve altogether. She strode the first few steps until the echoing of her footsteps on the stone floor became less pronounced as she walked across the hardwood. She stopped at her piano, let her eyes glance over the music that was still there, and she finally found the courage to turn around.

Everything was as it should be. Her house. Her door. Her life.

Why did it suddenly seem so much emptier? She hadn't thought it was possible for it to feel any emptier, but she was wrong. A familiar ache settled over her heart, but the origin of it was different.

With a sigh, she sat down on her piano bench and her eyes fell on the black fabric of the shirt she still wore. She fingered one of the sleeves and smiled. She brought it up to her nose and inhaled. Cedar and violin rosin.

A little of the sorrow in her heart lessened. It really had been *real*. No dream, no deluded fantasy. Liron was real. He existed. And if she had been able to go through the gateway once, she bet she could do it again.

But first, she needed to take care of her blaring alarm clock before her head exploded. And then, she was calling in to work. She was beyond exhausted.

Liron stared at the empty space where Melody's living room had been a moment ago. There was nothing now, just the vacant corner of his room. The popping and crackling of the logs in the fireplace seemed as loud as cannon blasts, echoing throughout the hollow room. His home had been silent before, lonely. Now it felt desolate.

Melody had only inhabited his life for a chaotic whirlwind of an evening, but she had left her impression upon him completely. Not only was she an anomaly for being able to traverse the continuum and come into his world, but she had done so willingly because she'd felt such a strong pull to him. And though she had been utterly terrified, she had put her faith and trust in him blindly. She had accepted his care and his touch in a way that defied logic for him. When every touch or every attempt at tenderness had been met with contempt and annoyance from Elizabeth, Melody had relished it, basked in it, sought it out.

There had been no other women for Liron before Elizabeth. Aside from the loving touch of his mother, he had never known a woman's warmth or caress. He'd ached for it from Elizabeth until her coldness had eradicated all hope of receiving kindness from her. And after she'd left, he had grown accustomed to his solitude. He couldn't believe how his heart had revived with just one trusting gesture from Melody. Her hand in his, her defense of him as he'd shared his story, the way she had flung herself into his arms when Siegfried had startled her, the way she'd allowed him to soothe her with his embrace and unique talent. All of those things made his heart rage and roar with fire he thought had long since died out.

It was an exquisite discovery, an enchanting, remarkable resurrection of his dormant heart. And for the short amount of time she had been with him, he had almost believed he could create music again. Because his music, written in his deepest pain, had touched her so much she'd been able to go against the laws of physics and reach him.

But now, she was gone. And the music was gone. All that was left was a lovely memory, a spilled bottle of wine on his floor, and a white shirt lying somewhere in his bedroom. He had been dangled beauty for one second, like bait from a hunter trying to snare a beast. Now, he was alone again. It startled him how much he yearned to feel her in his arms, to bury his face in her hair and see if it smelled like the sunlight it was kissed with.

He let out a defeated sigh and turned back into his room. Siegfried was perched atop one of the chairs, preening himself. Liron smiled, walked by the bird, and held his arm out. The falcon hopped up onto his forearm with a screech.

"I know, she interrupted your sleep. Come on, you cranky bird. Let's go to bed." He started back toward the hallway. "But for the record, you frightened her as much as she did you." He smiled to himself, remembering how she had leaned against him in the stairway. Perhaps she was gone, but he felt blessed to have had those moments with her at all. It had reminded him his heart still beat, that he was still a man, and that he was still alive.

Chapter Seven

Melody groaned and flopped the pillow down over her head to stifle the horrible blaring of her phone, which was almost as bad as the horrible blaring of her alarm. When it didn't stop, she crawled out from under the pillow and fumbled around on her nightstand until she managed to get the receiver out of the cradle. "What?" she grumbled.

"Geez, hello to you too," Nikki's voice came. "What are you doing? Were you asleep?"

"I was." Melody rolled over onto her back and rubbed her eyes.

"It's one o'clock in the afternoon. Are you sick?"

"No, I was just up late."

"Doing what?"

Melody sighed. "I couldn't sleep. I was having...weird dreams." It was close enough to the truth.

There was a pause on the other line. "Dreams? About what? Nightmares? Were they about your parents? Mel—"

Melody knew that tone in her friend's voice, and she was not in the mood for it. "Nikki, so help me, if you say, 'maybe you should see a therapist,' I *will* kill you. Or at the very least stop talking to you for about a week." She sat up and shoved her hand through her unruly and tangled mass of hair. She glanced down at the black shirt she still wore and smiled as she fingered the soft fabric. "And no, they weren't about my parents. They were just weird. I drank too much wine before I went to sleep."

"You were drinking? Why?"

Seriously? Did she have "basket case" written on her forehead? That was the only reason she could think of as to why everyone seemed to think she was one second away from insanity, or alcoholism, or any other psychological problem she could shake a stick at. "Because I made an Italian dinner and I felt like it. I'm twenty-seven years old. Do I need a note?"

"No, of course not. So, what were your dreams about?"

She's really not gonna let up, is she? "Space travel," she blurted. *There, that should do it.*

"Oh," Nikki said. "That's…interesting."

Melody smothered her laughter.

"Anyway, I'm sorry to wake you up. I was just in the mall shopping and I went to see you at work, but they told me you'd called in. I wanted to make sure you were okay."

Melody smiled at her friend's concern. "I'm fine, Nik. I just played hooky like when I was in high school."

Nikki giggled. "All right, well, go back to vegetating. I won't bug ya."

"Talk to you later, Nik." She hung up the phone and lay back against her pillows with a grin. She felt different than usual, not quite as depressed. Her heart didn't feel as heavy. And every time her mind wandered, it wandered right back to Liron, to his silky hair and luminous blue eyes. To his patient understanding and compassion. To the way he had cared for her and calmed her, held her. The way he had looked at her right before her alarm clock had brought them screaming back to reality.

She felt like a schoolgirl with a crush, and she didn't care. For the first time since her parents' death, she didn't feel like facing the day would be the equivalent of walking through molasses with cement shoes on.

She wondered what Liron was doing, if he was thinking of her, and if she would have the ability to travel to his world again if she tried. Deciding she had nothing better she wanted to do with her day, she swung her legs out of bed and headed to her closet. First things first, she was going to make sure she was not in her pajamas. If she managed to go through the gateway again, she wanted to at least look presentable. She maybe even felt like looking a little bit sexy.

After selecting an outfit that was casual, but still had a little bit of sass to it, she headed for the bathroom to take a nice, long shower.

It was around three o'clock when Melody was finally ready to sit down at her piano and see what kind of magic she could weave. She'd showered and made herself look decent in her good jeans and a black tank top with a sheer black blouse over it that came off the shoulders. It had tiny, shiny black beads interspersed throughout the fabric that sparkled in the right light. She'd pulled her hair up in a clip and left her bangs and some loose tendrils framing her face. She'd also put some makeup on, which was more than she usually did unless she had to go to work. Even when she'd gone out with Rob, she had only put on light foundation and some mascara. Today, she added a touch of smoky eye shadow, a soft, peachy blush, and some lip gloss.

She felt jittery, but in a good way, charged with adrenaline like when one was getting ready to go out on a date.

She stared at the music score for a while, wondering if the gateway would open again, hoping it would, and then wondering if she'd lost her mind. If she was any kind of practical, she would put the music away, be happy she'd made it back home at all, and would never again dabble with things she didn't understand about the universe. Obviously, she wasn't practical.

Sure, traveling to a different dimension unexpectedly had been horrifying. But when she'd gotten used to her surroundings, and learned more about Liron, the idea became more intriguing than scary. She wondered what other secrets the world had to offer.

She smiled and started to sit down on the piano bench when knocking sounded at her door. She instantly bristled. She did *not* want to deal with Rob right now. The man did not know when to quit.

Annoyed that he had interrupted her, and that she would probably need to blow him off her step with dynamite, she strode to the door and yanked it open.

Rob stood there with his sleazy grin, but it morphed into a look of shock when his gaze glanced over Melody. "Whoa," he murmured. His smile went from shocked, bypassed sleazy, and became demonic. "You got all dressed up for me. How did you know I was coming?"

She huffed and put her hand on her hip. A couple of silver bangles she'd placed around her wrist jangled with the action. "I did not dress up for you, Rob, and save your coercion tactics. I have a date." She got tremendous satisfaction out of his reaction. He looked like someone had just shot him in the butt.

"A date?" he snapped. "With who?"

She smirked. "With the man who wrote that music Nikki bought me."

It took him a couple minutes to actually figure out what she meant. She saw pain flash over his features from thinking too hard. "So, basically, you mean you're playing the piano all night again?" he grumbled. "You got dressed up to sit at the piano? How boring is that?"

She scowled. "I got dressed up because I wanted to. And sitting at my piano is what makes me happy. Just like target practice makes you happy." She rolled her eyes. "At any rate, I'm not free tonight."

She'd seen children who'd been spanked who didn't look as disgruntled at he did. "Great, now I'm being replaced by a musical instrument."

"Music was always first in my life, in case you didn't remember me telling you I was a musician."

"You said you *used* to be a musician."

She frowned and folded her arms. "I'm sorry, is my line of work going to be a problem for you? Because, by all means, go on back across the street. No one's forcing you to stay here." For some reason, she was having a difficult time finding the small smidgen of charm she usually found in Rob. He was annoying her, and all he cared about was himself. His interests, his wants.

"Dude, what is with the attitude lately, Mel? All I want to do is go on one stupid little date with you. You have something better to do? Besides plunk away on your keyboard?" He snorted. "Like *that's* a productive pastime."

Anger flared to life inside of Melody. How dare he insult her music? That was like insulting her soul, and insulting her parents as well. "All right, you've overstayed your welcome. If you really want to go out with me, I suggest leaving me be for a few days. Because, right now, all I really want to do is kick you in the nads." She grabbed hold of the inner door in one hand. "I'm not even addressing what you just said to me. And if you can't figure out why that upset me, you should probably never come back here again." She didn't wait for his response. She just shut the door. She didn't have time for this. *Arrogant, belligerent idiot....*

She went back to the piano, sat down, and started to pound out Liron's music. She used far too much force, fueled by her aggravation and imagining that all the keys were Rob's eyes she was poking out. She didn't do the music justice, blasting through it with the grace and skill of a buffalo.

When she got to the end of it, she looked over her shoulder, but saw nothing that was any different than her usual sofa, door, and walls. She heaved a sigh and let her shoulders slump as she turned back around. "Okay, Melody, get a grip," she muttered. She shook out her hands to release tension, cracked her neck, and poised her fingers back over the keys.

She thought of Liron's eyes, his touch, his kind attentiveness and subtle, graceful sensuality. She remembered how he had infused her with music while he had held her protectively in his arms.

Slowly, she began to play the music the way it was intended to be played, and she was swept away within the beautiful notes once again.

The castle looked different in the light of day than it had the night before. Sunlight streamed through the stained glass windows, casting rainbows across the stone. Outside, she could hear the crashing of the ocean waves. "Liron?" she called, excited that she had managed to open the gateway again. It was a cool power to be able to have, traveling between dimensions. She wasn't sure how she would get back home again, but eventually, something would trigger the portal, as her alarm clock had done before. Right now, she wasn't really that concerned. She felt drudgery when she was home. A house full of painful memories, a job she abhorred, and an irritating man who didn't know how to take no for an answer. Liron had made her feel more warmth in one night than she had experienced in over a year. His world was different, and was not marred by things that would only remind her of hurt.

"Liron?" she called again, stepping further into the room to look around. "Liron, where are you?"

He suddenly rounded the corner, looking shocked and slightly bewildered. "Melody," he murmured. "You came back."

She grinned, her heart beating wildly at his presence, and especially at the way his gaze raked over her. "I wanted to see if I could," she said, hooking her thumbs in her belt loops and rocking on the balls of her feet. She shrugged. "Besides, I wanted to see you again." She admitted it quietly and chewed on her bottom lip.

He stared at her for a second, his eyes full of surprise and so much warmth she felt herself blush.

He stepped toward her and let his eyes appraise her before they came up to meet hers. "You look breathtaking."

"Better than wine-soaked PJs, right?" she teased.

He smiled. "You looked beautiful even in that, but today..." He shook his head. "What is the occasion?"

There was a hint of playfulness in his eyes and his tone, so she went with it. "Coming to see you, you idiot." She put her hand on her hip in mock annoyance. "You're going to take me on a date."

He raised an eyebrow. "Am I?" He folded his arms across his chest, continuing the game.

She gave a flippant shrug. "Well, if you don't want to, fine. I'll just go back home. I'm sure Rob would be more than thrilled for me to give him another shot." She pivoted on her heel with a snotty air and turned to face the far side of his living room. Lots of gray stone met her gaze and she chewed on her bottom lip with a frown. "As soon as I figure out how..."

His rich chuckle heated her blood and he came up behind her, placing his hands on her bare shoulders and letting his fingers trail tantalizingly down her arms. Feather-soft notes filled her mind and tingles exploded across her skin. "It seems you have encountered a problem." He whispered it against her ear, and her heart tumbled over itself as his breath tickled the hair at the nape of her neck. "And I am not terribly pleased with the idea of this Rob fellow."

She grinned and leaned back toward him instinctively. "Then do something about it."

He laughed softly and moved away. She turned around to face him, and he offered her his arm in a very old world, gentlemanly gesture. "Shall we?"

Chapter Eight

Melody had been to the ocean once when she was small. Her parents had taken her to Disneyland and they'd spent a day at the beach. She had enjoyed playing in the waves and building sandcastles. But the Southern California coast was nothing like what she was currently looking at. There were no sunbathers or surfers here. No one playing beach volleyball. There was hardly any beach at all. Only craggy cliffs and jagged rock that the waves flung themselves against, sending salty spray and foam into the air.

This ocean was angry, violent, powerful, and bewitching. It was so much more dramatic than what she had seen as a child. She wished her parents could have seen it. It was nature's symphony, as Liron had said. She knew her mother and father would have heard it too, and would have loved to share in the wondrous crescendo each wave built before breaking into the rock.

"Have you always loved the sea?" she asked Liron, turning her head to look at him over her shoulder. He stood stoically behind her, allowing her space with her thoughts.

They had left his home to come walking down here, and she was surprised at how ordinary everything looked. She didn't know what she had been expecting. Green men and a pink sun maybe...something much more befitting inter-dimensional travel. But the sky was still blue. The grass was still green. And this ocean was the most magnificent thing she had ever seen.

Liron stepped closer until he was standing beside her and he nodded. "I grew up here, played along these rocks. I have never had any desire to live anywhere else. Elizabeth hated it." He looked down and shrugged. "Said the noise kept her awake and the salt in the air bothered her skin."

Melody rolled her eyes. "What a hag."

Liron chuckled and gave her a sidelong glance. "I am curious to see how many names you can come up with for my ex-wife."

"Oh, I have plenty," she grumbled. "How could anyone not fall in love with this?" She stretched her arms out to indicate the breathtaking expanse before her.

"I spent a lot of time asking myself that. As well as how come she could never fall in love with me."

"Because she was blind, deaf, dumb, and stupid."

He raised an eyebrow. "How do you figure?"

"Well, any woman with half a brain can see that you're super hot, so there's the dumb and blind part." She glanced at him and saw him smile shyly while his face flushed a faint shade of pink. She grinned. His bashfulness was a refreshing change from Rob's arrogance. "You worshipped the ground she walked on, and any woman who could turn her nose up at that is friggin' stupid. Plus,"—she held her arms out again and shook them for emphasis—"look at this! How could she *not* hear the music in this? It's like the most extraordinary concerto ever created, only better because it's pure. No man-made composition could ever compare to the perfection of this. You could spend a lifetime trying to put notes to it to describe it, and it would always, always fall short." She shook her head and closed her eyes, breathing deep and letting her ears fill with the melodies only someone with true musical aptitude and appreciation could hear.

When she opened her eyes and looked at him, she found him regarding her thoughtfully with admiration and wonder reflected in his blue depths.

"What?" she questioned.

"You have such a complete understanding and deep love of music."

She smiled even though a pang of grief stabbed through her heart. "Both my parents were musicians. My mom, a violinist, and my dad, a cellist. I grew up listening to Sibelius and Vivaldi. 'Pachelbel in D' was what my mother hummed to me when I was a child, and if there was ever a Saturday that I *didn't* wake up to my father playing cello until all his bow hair fell out, I knew he was either out of town or had the flu." She gave a little laugh at the memories, regardless of the ache they created in her heart. "Needless to say, I didn't stand much of chance. By the time I graduated high school, I was accomplished at piano, flute, and viola, and I could pick my way through some stuff on the guitar." He smirked and she shrugged. "I dated a rocker guy for a little while."

He grinned. "If I didn't know better, I would think you had been raised by muses."

She shook her head and averted her gaze back out to the sea, remembering her parents and the wonderful years she had spent with them. "No...just two incredibly talented people." She couldn't mistake the sadness in her voice, and she knew Liron heard it too.

"Have you always been a musician then?" he queried.

She nodded and forced a small smile. "I loved music as much as they did. We all played in an orchestra together. I was working on a concerto for a while, but...." She shrugged and let the sentence remain unformed.

"Melody." His voice was a velvet sweep of sound that caressed over her in a wave of sinful warmth. "What happened?"

She chewed on her bottom lip and looked up at him, a torturous sorrow welling up within her until her chest felt like it would shatter into pieces from the enormity of the pressure. "They died last year in a car accident." She felt the tears burn, but she knew they would never fall.

He stepped forward with no hesitation and placed his hands on her shoulders, gently rubbing up and down in a comforting gesture.

"I was working on a concerto for the orchestra, one that would have featured all of us. But I haven't been able to look at it since. I hadn't even played piano until my friend Nikki brought me your music. Your piece is the first thing I've played since the morning before the accident."

He sighed and pulled her into the refuge of his embrace, which immediately surrounded her in warm, wonderful notes. "I'm sorry, Melody. That kind of loss is something I cannot comprehend and makes my grief over Elizabeth seem childish and silly."

She shook her head in disagreement as she nestled deeper into his arms, relishing the strength that he provided. "Loss is loss, Liron. One should not be compared with the other. And it was your loss I identified with, that I heard within the notes of that score. However twisted it sounds, your loss was what called out to me, and what I reached out for last night when I was playing. Your pain took my mind off of mine. All I wanted to do was soothe the ache I felt in that song."

He pulled away enough to look down at her, and he took her face in his hands, lifting it so he could gaze into her eyes. "Why would you want to do that? You didn't know I was real."

"No, but I knew the music had an origin, and I didn't think anyone else should have to feel the same kind of heartache I did."

He stared at her for a long moment, several undecipherable emotions flashing through his eyes. Slowly, he extended his fingers across her jaw, behind her ears and to the clip that held her hair captive. "Then the pain Elizabeth caused me when she left was really a gift in disguise," he murmured. Deftly, he unclasped her clip and her hair tumbled down and around her shoulders in thick waves, unruly with the sea breeze.

"What do you mean?" She frowned.

He buried his fingers in her hair and trailed them through the length. "I wrote that music because I wanted her to know the pain she caused by leaving me, the devotion and longing I still had for her. Somehow, that music survived all these years and touched something within you. That, in turn, brought you to me." His eyes met hers with intensity, with meaning and sincerity. "And that is truly, above all other things, a gift."

She closed her eyes for a moment, basking in the feel of his gentle fingers in her hair. Even that simple touch made her hear low, tinkling bells. She pressed closer to him, her lonely, broken heart craving the kindness that he offered so freely. She smiled a little as her senses filled with the smell of the sea, the feel of Liron standing so close to her, his hands in her hair, his music in her mind. She heard the cry of seagulls and the thunder of the waves. The heat of his body permeated hers, and the warmth of his soul reached her cold, shattered heart.

He trailed his lips in a line of tender kisses from her cheek to her temple. Butterflies took flight in her stomach while infernal heat exploded through her body. Nothing she had ever experienced felt as good as being close to him.

Liron was gentle strength and patient compassion all wrapped up in wondrous music. He was everything she cherished, admired, and craved.

"Melody," he whispered, his breath against her ear causing her to shiver. "Do you have anything pressing that will cause your world to come crashing back into mine and take you away again?"

She smiled and slipped an arm around his neck to fit them closer together. "Not that I can think of. And even if something, or someone, tried to interrupt, I have the ability to ignore the portal and not go back through it."

One of his hands stayed in her hair while the other one traveled over her shoulder and down her spine to rest at her lower back. "Good. Because I find myself unwilling to part with you at the moment."

She giggled and pulled back just enough to be able to look at him. He was smiling, and her heart sighed. "I don't think I mind."

His smile blossomed into a ravenously beautiful grin, and she leaned back into his body, craving his touch and transfixed with his perfect mouth. She remembered the night before, how close they had come to kissing. What would she have to do to get him to try again? The way his eyes smoldered, she didn't think he would need too much convincing. Heck, with the way her body smoldered, *she* might be the one to make the first move.

But before either of them could do anything, a shrill cry sounded from above and drew Liron's attention away from her. He stepped back and held his arm out as a large, golden falcon swooped down and landed on it. Liron smiled and reached his other hand up to smooth the bird's feathers. "Let us have a more formal introduction," he said. "Melody, meet Siegfried." He stepped closer and extended his arm out to her. "Go on, he won't hurt you. He's all noise and sass."

Melody giggled and reached out to trail her fingers gently across his wings. "I don't know. I think he may have been jealous of how close I was to you," she teased.

Liron looked up at her, his eyes burning. "He'll just have to learn to share."

His words made her heartbeat falter, and she took in the beauty of the moment, the beauty of him. Standing there, his dark hair blowing gently in the breeze, a large bird of prey perched on his arm, with the roiling, tempestuous sea as his backdrop, Liron was beyond beautiful, beyond breathtaking. He was beyond anything she had ever imagined.

His smile lit up her whole being. "Would you like to see more of my world?" he invited. "I did promise you a date after all." The wicked gleam in his eye was sexy on a whole new level.

When Rob had bullied her into the several dates they had gone on, Melody had always felt this sort of obligatory acceptance. But she'd known in the back of her mind that at the end of it, she would be left feeling drained, unsatisfied, and annoyed. She was thrilled at the possibility of spending the evening with Liron, experiencing this extraordinary world and learning more about the man who brought to life so much music and so much feeling within her that she had thought long gone.

The whole last year of her life she had been searching for a distraction, something to take her mind off of the empty, gaping hole her parents' death had left in her heart. Liron didn't distract her, didn't fill her mind with useless things that would make her forget about music. Liron *was* music. Every inch of his being was etched from it. If anything, his presence should have been painful, a constant reminder of what she had lost. But it wasn't. It was soothing and soft, a gentle, prodding remembrance of why she had fallen in love with music in the first place.

Music heals. Art heals.

Her father had said it countless times. But she had turned her back on that truth because surviving through the pain to find the healing on the other side had been too difficult.

"Melody?" She glanced up at Liron, who was looking at her in concern. He sent Siegfried back up into the sky and reached out to her. "Are you all right?"

She sighed and made herself smile. "I'm fine."

He arched an eyebrow, and she knew he didn't believe her at all, but he didn't push the subject. Instead, he took her hand in his and brought her wrist to his lips, kissing the inside of it with so much kindness her blood turned to lava, her heart threatened to burst, and the most amazing notes and chords exploded within her mind.

Before she knew what she was doing, she was back in his arms, clutching onto him with a desperation that was not like her. Her fingers dug into his back, and her body trembled with the weight of her emotions. She squeezed her eyes shut and buried her face against his chest, trying to find sanctuary in his warmth, his smell, and the music that made up who he was. Music was the one thing that had never abandoned her, even when she had tried to abandon it. It stayed with her even now, in every beat of Liron's magnificent heart.

"Liron," she whispered. "Please, show me your world. Just keep me here and away from my world. It's a cold, bleak place. All I know is pain there, sorrow and loneliness. I don't want to feel that anymore. I want to hear music again."

His arms tightened around her and he held her close. "It's not your world that is bleak, Melody," he murmured against her hair. "It's only a place, just as this is only a place. It's your heart that is cold and lonely. I know because mine has been also. I, too, want to hear music again."

She looked up at him, knowing her eyes had to look desperate and lost. "I want to forget," she all but pleaded. "Please, help me forget."

The blue of his eyes turned darker with sincere understanding. "I can't make you forget, Melody. Even if you try and succeed for a time, the pain you are running from will always be there, waiting to attack you when you least expect it." He shook his head and framed her face with his hands. "All you can do is move forward. You will never hear music as you once did, but that does not mean it can't be just as beautiful in a different way." He cupped her jaw in his palm and feathered his thumb across her cheek. "I heard nothing for many, many years after Elizabeth left me. I feared I would never hear anything again. I figured she had destroyed my ability to do so. I never thought it would return to me in the form of a crashing, shrieking, frightened woman who had accidentally transported herself into my living room and kept insisting I was a hallucination."

Melody laughed in spite of herself.

Liron smiled. "Nevertheless, I heard the music all the same. It came rushing back to me with your trust, your care, your blind faith in me and my ability to keep you safe. I realized last night after you returned to your home, that music, like all art and all things creative, is eternal. It is a gift to hear the beauty you and I do. It is a gift to feel it as we do. It, like emotion, may change shape. Its notes may become different because of what we experience. A different instrument may be required to convey meanings that maybe were not there before. But, like a shadow, it is always there. It is always within us. You just have to find strength enough to listen, and not be afraid of what it may sound like."

Melody stared up at him, enraptured and mesmerized. The truth in his words made her heart shiver. And the way he looked at her...it set her body aflame and cocooned her in compassion all at the same time. It was a heady, drugging sensation and she wanted more of him. More of his touch, more of his words, more of his wisdom and his care.

She shook her head, and he frowned.

"What?" he questioned with a skeptical look.

"Your ex-wife really was a psycho hose beast."

He blinked in bewilderment. "A what?"

"Psycho hose beast. You know, from *Wayne's World*?"

"Wayne's what?"

She rolled her eyes and waved her hand. "It's a movie. Never mind. She was a jerk. And I think maybe I hate her."

He chuckled and his arms around her tightened, causing his hips to press against hers in an intimate way that made her brain spin around in her skull. "I don't. Her stolen music score brought me you."

"You keep saying that."

"I keep meaning it."

She smiled and rested her cheek against his chest for a moment, listening to his heart as it matched the pounding of the ocean waves. His arms were the most tranquil place she had been since her parents had died. Every time he held her, she felt like she could finally rest.

"Psycho hose beast," he muttered. "That doesn't even make sense."

She laughed and grinned up at him. "Sure it does. She sucked the life out of you. Like a vacuum. A hose. You know?"

His eyebrows drew together in a kind of pained expression. "Maybe I will keep you here. The popular culture and urban slang of your world is...."

She nodded while he searched for the words. "I know. It

makes your IQ drop a couple points." He smirked and she toyed with the buttons of his shirt. "Show me your world, Liron. Show me everything."

"That might take a while," he said with a soft laugh.

She ran her palms up his chest and knew she'd never meant anything so much as what she was about to say, regardless of how irrational it was. Her pain was less when she was with Liron. It was less because he understood in a way no one at home possibly could. He didn't make her feel stupid, or like she needed to get a grip. He didn't give her that concerned for her sanity look like Nikki did. He just listened, and held her, and calmed her with music when things became too overwhelming.

Music. The only language she had ever really been good at. The only therapy that had ever worked.

Reaching up to tuck back a strand of his hair, she murmured, "I might be inclined to stay."

Chapter Nine

Liron was in danger. Serious danger.

He watched as Melody wandered through the market-place, awestruck, her eyes filled with wonderment. He looked down at where her fingers were twined with his. She had been holding his hand since they'd left the cliffs, as if she didn't want to be too far from him. Every time they severed the connection for her to look at a vendor's wares, she sought his touch again as soon as she had finished.

The things she brought to life within him made what he felt for Elizabeth when he'd first met her seem trivial. He had been blown away by her beauty and her grace, by the music he had heard when he'd looked at her. But he had never been able to explore his feelings for her. She had never let him. He had been in love with a possibility that had never become a reality.

But Melody… She was completely different. She seemed to seek his touch, his presence. She had come back to him, even though she had been so unsettled by her unexpected journey into his world. She had returned because she had *wanted to*, not out of obligation. Not because she'd had no other choice. She had desired his world, his company. She had desired him. It was a simple thing, he imagined, but held so much force it rocked the very core of him.

She understood his nature, what made him who he was. She understood music with a depth he had never experienced from anyone other than another musical muse. And they shared the same pain, that same empty, aching loss. They both knew what it was like to have their inspiration die. His loneliness had brought her to him, and as a result, they had both rediscovered music in each other.

He was in danger of wanting her so completely he feared he would never be the same.

But he couldn't help but think that maybe that was a good thing. The fear he should have felt, the trepidation, wasn't there. His broken and bruised heart felt comfortable with Melody. Safe. And for the first time ever, he felt like maybe he could move past hope, past a possibility, and learn what it was like to share himself with another.

Maybe....

Twilight had descended as the two of them had spent several hours perusing the wares of the vendors and traders in the marketplace. The shopkeepers started to close up their booths, much to Melody's dismay, and Liron led her down the street. "In several hours the marketplace will be alive again, with a different kind of entertainment," he said with a smile. "But until then, would you like some dinner?" He stopped outside the door of one of the more reputable taverns.

She glanced up at the sign, then put one hand on her hip and cocked her head in a playful, flirty gesture. "You know, Rob has taken me to dinner a couple times at a few really upscale places, and the feeling I've generally had when I've gone has been slight nausea, despite the delicious food. Now, I'm standing outside some seedy tavern, and I really can't wait to find out what's on the menu." One of her eyebrows arched up in a teasing expression. "I'm beginning to think maybe my problem was the company."

He narrowed his eyes and feigned irritation. "Who is this man you keep referring to? He sounds rather unpleasant, and I don't think I like the fact that he keeps making an appearance in our conversation."

Her laughter lightened his heart in a way he had seldom experienced. Knowing he had been the one to cause it made it that much more magical. "What's wrong, Liron? Do you feel threatened?" She came up close to him, her eyes seducing him with their burning sensuality.

His insides ignited. The fact that she asked, that the possibility even entered her mind, meant that she acknowledged the mutual attraction between them. It was difficult not to. Sexual tension arced between them like electricity. Every time she came near him, his body reminded him of how completely un-dormant he was.

He buried his hands in her hair, relishing the silken strands as they slipped through his fingers. "And if I do?"

She ran her palms up his chest again in the way that made his knees want to give out every time she did it. "Don't be."

Her tempting lips were turned up to him, beckoning, pleading for him to claim them with his. For one horrible moment, he wondered if he would even remember how to kiss a woman. It had been so bloody long.

He had loved Elizabeth instantly. And he was horribly infatuated with this woman. Apparently, his heart's idea of playing it safe was waiting a night before deciding it wanted to hand itself over to a woman. Every second he was with Melody, every teasing glance she shot him, every piece of spunk, every time she ran her palms across his chest the way she liked to do, he stumbled more and more into frightening territory.

He wanted to guard his heart, wanted to be safe, aloof. But he couldn't.

Not when she made him hear rhapsodies.

He lowered his lips toward hers, aching to sample her taste, feel the petal softness of her mouth against his. It was an all-consuming desire. One he was powerless to resist.

She tilted her face up to his, accepting, welcoming....

"Hold your horses! I have to go and feed the pigs if you want to stay in business, you lazy scoundrel!"

A large woman with a bosom that could have swallowed a small child burst out of the tavern door, carrying a pan full of hog slop. She was too busy yelling over her shoulder at the "lazy scoundrel" to see Liron and Melody, who were positioned in a rather bad place directly in her path. Liron saw what was coming, and tried to move Melody out of the way, but his reflexes were not as quick as he might have hoped, and the woman was an unstoppable force.

She ceased shouting long enough to turn around and plow straight into Melody, overturning the pan, which cascaded down the front of her splendid outfit.

Melody shrieked and stumbled back, then looked down at her shirt and pants in horror.

"Madam, I'm so sorry!" the woman cried. "I wasn't paying attention to where I was going!"

Melody let out a wavering, shaky sound and turned her attention to Liron. "Why?" she muttered. "Seriously...*why*?"

He grimaced and went to her. "Melody, I am so very sorry. It was my fault for stopping in the doorway."

Her shock slowly transformed into agitation, and she shook her arms sharply. "Why do I seem to be spending my time with you covered in liquids?" she snapped.

"Please, let me get you a change of clothes," the woman said, flitting and fussing over Melody in a way that was really no help whatsoever. "My daughter is very slim, as you are. I am sure you can fit into something of hers. Please, I am so sorry, madam. Come inside and I will tend to this." She took Melody's hand and started to tug her in the direction of the tavern. "Dinner is on the house as well. I insist."

Melody shot a scathing scowl over her shoulder at Liron as she stiffly followed after the woman. Liron trailed after them into the tavern and up the stairs. The woman ushered Melody into a room where there was a heated argument for several moments between the tavern owner and another girl, presumably her daughter, before the owner came out again and all but fled down the stairs.

"Gwennie will see to your lady, sir!" she shouted back at him as she hurried away. "And I will tell my husband to cook you the finest steak chili. We just slaughtered a cow this morning!"

Liron blinked, then sighed and leaned back against the wall to wait, much like he had done the night before. He had only been standing there for maybe ten minutes at the most when the door flew open again and a young girl stormed out looking irate.

She faced him and stabbed her finger in the direction of the room. "Go and tend to your lady!" she commanded.

Liron arched an eyebrow and stood up straight. "I beg your pardon?"

She huffed and shoved a strand of her sandy hair off of her freckled face. "I'm not trying to be rude here, but I can't sit around and dote on her because my mother is a clod. I have things to do!" She glanced at the stairs, then sidled up to Liron and spoke behind her hand in a hushed tone. "I have *a man* to do."

He frowned and stared at her for a few seconds. "That was...entirely too much unnecessary information," he stated.

She rolled her eyes and spun toward the stairs. "I laid out

some clothing for her. So just do what you need to do and let yourself out." She rushed down the staircase.

Liron stared after her, then heaved a sigh and opened the door. He strode in and stopped short at seeing a tub in the center of the room, with a scowling Melody in it. A scowling, *naked* Melody. He squeezed his eyes shut and turned his head to the side as the door swung closed behind him. "Oh, good lord!" he cried.

"Well, gee, Liron. That's *just* the kind of reaction I was hoping for." Her voice was saturated in aggravated sarcasm.

"Forgive me, I didn't know.... I mean—the girl...." He felt like a blabbering fool. "She never said...." He huffed. "I'm sorry. I will wait outside and let you dry off. She didn't tell me you were...indisposed." He turned.

"Liron, gimme a break. What are you, twelve? I know what parts I have and so do you. I don't care! Just get me a freaking towel so I can get out of this freaking tub!"

He swallowed once, twice, and then somehow managed to gather the strength to be able to open his eyes and turn to look at her while keeping his body in check.

It was a monumental task.

Sure, he knew all about female anatomy. That did not mean that he was great at getting his male anatomy to co-operate when he was suddenly thrown right in front of a wet, naked woman who he so happened to be horribly attracted to. Gentleman or not, he was still a man. Certain things were just biological.

He stifled a groan as he stepped toward her and grabbed the towel that had been placed on a chair just out of her reach. "How come they decided to bathe you?" he asked, chancing a glance up at her. *Just look into her eyes. Look into her eyes.*

Her eyes were very unamused.

"Well, because. I had hog slop running down my cleavage, so there was that."

A laugh was torn from him at her curt tone, and he handed the towel out to her, averting his eyes as she stood up and stepped out of the tub. He grasped another towel and turned back to her once she had wrapped the first one around herself. His heart softened. She looked bedraggled and war-torn. Her eye makeup had run tracks down her cheeks and her lustrous blonde hair was damp and stringy.

He smiled and guided her to sit on the edge of the tub. Then, he took the towel he held and started to gently wipe the rogue makeup off of her cheeks.

She made a small, growling noise in the back of her throat. "I don't even want to know what I look like. Those women practically stripped me and shoved me into that tub."

He chuckled and tipped her chin up so he could get the black from under her eyes. They captured him and some of the irritation in them warmed into a slow-burning desire. His gaze traveled from her eyes to her lips, full and soft and begging for attention. He lowered his head toward her, abandoning the process of wiping off her makeup. She slid her hands up the front of his chest, encouraging him, drawing him closer.

He closed his eyes and took her face in his hands, leaning forward and down to reach her lips, which had become the object of his obsession over the past twenty-four hours. She tilted her chin up to him, welcoming his advance.

She wavered beneath his touch and let out a startled shriek as she started to lose her balance and tilt backward. Reflexively, she grasped a handful of his shirt to steady herself, and succeeded in pulling him so far forward he couldn't catch himself in time. He barely had a chance to shout before he toppled over her and sent them both over the edge of the tub and back into the lukewarm water.

Melody got the worst of it, being completely submerged under his body weight while he flailed around like a fish out of water trying to right himself. He flipped over so as not to drown her and landed in the water backside first with his legs curling over the side of the tub. Melody emerged, coughing and sputtering, looking more despondent than the first time.

They looked at one another, and Liron suppressed a wince, sure she was going to be furious at him. But to his surprise, a warm smile curved her lips and she started to laugh softly. "I'm beginning to think kissing you is a bad idea."

He chuckled and shook his head. He extracted himself from the tub and reached a hand out to help her out as well. As she stood, the towel she had been wearing slipped off in a waterlogged heap, and he squeezed his eyes shut with a groan he couldn't have contained if he'd tried.

To Melody's credit, she didn't razz him about it. She moved around him while he strategically kept his eyes closed, passing with a soft touch on his arm.

A few seconds later, an aggravated curse drew his attention, followed by her exclaimed, "Are you freaking kidding me?"

He opened his eyes and turned to where she stood in a skimpy, two-piece, purple outfit he usually only saw belly dancers wear. Tiny silver bells adorned the flimsy, sheer skirt and tinkled when Melody moved.

For a moment, as his body flamed beyond a temperature he thought was healthy, he wondered if maybe having her in this outfit was worse than having her naked.

"What is this all about?" she cried in obvious exasperation.

He swallowed hard and tried to tear his attention away from her flat, toned stomach. "The girl who assisted you must be a dance muse," he responded absently while his gaze traveled from her stomach down to her long legs barely visible through the gauzy skirt.

"Well la-dee-da!" she cried. "I'm not an anything muse and I look like some sort of gypsy hooker!"

He chuckled and moved forward to take her hands in his and draw her close. "I have seen many women in my time," he murmured against her ear. "And never have they made me burn the way you do." He pressed a gentle kiss to her jawline before pulling back to look into her eyes. "You do *not* look like a gypsy hooker." She let out a disgruntled growl, and he reached up to push a few damp strands of hair off of her face. "If it makes you feel any better whatsoever, my entire midsection is soaked through."

She glanced down at the band of wet across his torso and hips and giggled.

He shook his head and held his hand out to her. "This is hardly what I had in mind when I decided to take you on your date."

She grinned and placed her delicate hand in his. Long, slender fingers, a true musician's hand. "What, you mean an absent-minded woman spilling hog slop all down my shirt, an irritated girl stripping me and shoving me into a bathtub, you attempting to be suave and kiss me only to fall into the tub yourself and try to drown me, and me getting stuck in some atrocious belly dancing costume for the rest of the evening wasn't your idea of a romantic time?"

He chuckled. "Well, when you put it that way, it is a bit of an adventure, isn't it?"

"Definitely more of an adventure than I've had in a while."

He squeezed her fingers and led her out of the room. "Come on. I was promised the best steak chili this establishment has to offer on the house. At least we got that out of the deal."

She whimpered and held back. He glanced at her over his shoulder in concern.

"Do I really have to go out there in this?"

He allowed his gaze to sweep appraisingly over her once again. "Melody, what are you worried about? You look so amazing I can't keep my eyes on you for too long or else my mind will become filled with dark, wicked notes."

Her eyes filled with something warm and sensual at his words, and she moved to place her arm around his waist and snuggle against his side. "Okay, but only you can hear that kind of music when you look at me. If anyone else does, I'm gonna kick them in the head."

He laughed softly and pulled her close against him. "I fully support that plan." He pressed a kiss to the top of her head, then continued to lead them out of the room. The fact that he heard music at all when he looked at her was amazing. He had not heard anything in so long. She inspired him the way he was supposed to inspire humans, the way a muse mate was supposed to inspire another muse. The things he heard rivaled what he had heard when he'd loved Elizabeth.

He knew it was possible for a muse and a human to be mated, but he had not imagined that the inspiration would be the same. Now that he knew it could be, or could possibly be more powerful than a muse/muse mating, he didn't want to think about what it would be like when Melody decided to go back to her own world. A horrendous, torturous pain filled his heart when he let his mind travel to that inevitability.

Had Elizabeth felt that for her human? What she had felt had to have been strong enough for her to transcend the boundary between the two realms and exist within the human world. If she had felt even remotely for her human what Liron was beginning to feel for Melody, he could almost understand why she had done what she had.

Almost.

Stealing his music was still an underhanded thing he couldn't quite get over. But loving someone... He was starting to realize he had loved the idea of Elizabeth more than he had loved the person. What was blossoming inside of him for Melody was so much stronger and so much more powerful.

He didn't want to consider the possibility of her leaving, even though he knew she had to eventually. When she did, he wondered if he would desire to remain in his realm at all. He really had nothing there. If he decided he wanted to come back to her world with her, would she welcome him?

His emotions were surging so fast, it was impossible to decipher them all. Accompanied with the influx of music he heard and felt within him when he had heard nothing for so long, his insides felt like a raging typhoon. It would be a miracle if he survived all of this.

But as he glanced down at Melody, at her hand placed trustingly in his as he guided her down the staircase and into the main hall of the tavern, he wondered if he wanted to survive. A huge part of him wanted to be lost to her for all time.

That was the part that frightened him.

Chapter Ten

Melody watched in rapt fascination as the marketplace came alive with the set of the sun. While she and Liron had eaten dinner inside of the tavern, the merchants had closed up shop and performers of all sorts had made the marketplace their stage.

The steak chili they had eaten had been wonderful. Not quite worth getting hog slop dumped on her and being forced into a belly dancing costume, but wonderful nonetheless. She and Liron had shared amazing conversation about music, and as soon as they had finished, he had brought her back out here to witness the festivities.

Melody had never seen anything like it in her life. It was as if she had fallen into *A Midsummer Night's Dream* or something else just as whimsical. Musicians played a variety of instruments ranging from violins and cellos to flutes, bagpipes, guitars, and drums, while dancers of all kinds, both men and women, lost themselves within the music in the middle of the marketplace square. Most of them were dressed as she was, in scarves and bells, like some kind of throwback to the Celtic and gypsy world, but others were dressed in things closer to leotards while their dancing resembled the modern, lyrical dance of her era. Others, loners, sat around on the outskirts scribbling on paper with quill pens, and a group of scholarly men and women off in the distance argued and debated about something they were apparently very vehement about. Some joined the musicians with their lovely soprano and baritone voices, and others sat scattered around drawing or painting on easels. Fire jugglers also took up space amidst the dancers, garbed in menacing black and silver, like gothic art. Some of them had face piercings and intricate tattoos.

She shook her head in wonderment as she took it all in, and from where she sat on the edge of a fountain, she felt Liron's hand encompass hers. She glanced at him over her shoulder and smiled.

His eyes were warm and sparkling. "What do you think?"

"This is amazing," she murmured. "So much wonderful talent. Do they do this every night?"

He nodded. "It's how we express ourselves. Muses are born to express their talent. We don't know any other way to be."

"Have you ever done this?" She pointed over toward the free-for-all happening in front of her.

He smiled almost shyly. "I used to. Long ago."

The wistfulness in his voice, the note of aching longing, made a pain work its way through her heart. "What kind of muses are these?" she asked. "Obviously, those are music muses, like you." She pointed to the group of musicians.

"Yes, and those are dance muses, and voice muses, and art muses." He indicated the singers, dancers, and painters.

"What about those?" She pointed to the loners who were writing.

"Those are writing and lyric muses. They generally keep to themselves, writing their poetry and verse, their fiction, amidst the chaos, but not taking an active part in it."

"What about them?" She pointed to the group of debaters.

"Most of them are science and logic muses."

She raised an eyebrow. "You have muses for logic?"

He nodded with a smile. "And philosophy. They argue all the time. Very annoying to have at parties."

She giggled. "Okay, what about them?" She pointed to the fire dancers.

His smile morphed into a mischievous grin. "Isn't it obvious? They are rebel muses."

She blinked at him for a second while her mind tried to process the information. "*Rebel* muses? Are you trying to tell me that there is a muse devoted entirely to chaos and mayhem?"

He shrugged lazily. "Of course. Where would the excitement in life come from if there wasn't any of that?"

She laughed. "So, pretty much, all of the tattoo artists, bikers, and metal heads in my world are inspired by rebel muses?"

"It is a possibility." His smile disarmed her, and all she wanted to do was kiss him until he was gasping for breath.

Her brazen, dominant desire was foreign to her, but not un-welcome. She had spent so much of the last year feeling lost. Knowing what she wanted, what she ached for, was a nice change of pace.

She turned her attention back to the performers, enjoy-ing how free they all seemed. It was not so different from how she had felt as a child when she'd watched her parents rehearse with the orchestra. How many nights had she spent in the theatre, watching in fascination as the musicians lost themselves amidst the notes they created? She missed that feeling, that abandon.

She glanced down at the atrocious costume she had been placed in, then over at the other women who were dressed the same. They owned their attire, dancing and twirling and laughing as if they had no cares whatsoever. What did that feel like, she wondered?

"So, what's stopping you?" she asked, flashing Liron a teasing smile.

He arched an eyebrow. "From what?"

She pointed over at the mass of performers.

"You want me to play something?" To her surprise, his voice only held the faintest note of confusion. Beneath that, he sounded extremely serious, almost like he had been wait-ing for the invitation.

She grinned. "I would love that."

The smile that lit his face should have brought golden light cascading around the whole marketplace square, and warmth stole throughout her entire body, gentle and com-forting around her heart and spanning out to smolder every-where else.

He stood and arched an eyebrow in a playful expression. "I almost wonder if I remember how."

She giggled, and he winked at her before striding over to the group of musicians. They paused in their playing as he approached, causing all of the dancers to take a breather as well. They spoke for a while until one of the men handed Liron his acoustic guitar. Liron slipped the strap over his shoulders, then took a viola that was being offered to him and turned back to Melody. He motioned her over and indi-cated the instrument.

Melody's stomach lurched and she stared at him for a

minute, then pointed to herself in question.

He nodded with a chuckle. "You told me you could play viola. If I'm going to do this, so are you."

Her first reaction was to kill him, but she couldn't stay annoyed when he was beaming at her like that. Of course, he had to pick the viola. She hadn't touched one in years. Piano was her instrument of choice. Apprehension flooded her as she hesitantly made her way over to him.

"Liron, I haven't played one of these in so long...." Even as she said it, she took the instrument anyway. "Can't you give me a drum to bang on instead? I think I could manage that." She glanced around at the other musicians and swallowed hard. "I'm not equipped with your kind of...talents." She was a regular old human, nothing muse-like about her at all. She'd be lucky if she managed to produce some kind of awful screech.

Liron shook his head. "Melody, play whatever you like. You start and we will follow you."

She stared at him for a second, dumbfounded, then snorted. "Yeah, sure, no pressure." She raised the instrument to her shoulder and blundered her way through the only piece of music she could remember, some middle section of "Russian Sailor's Dance" by R. Gliere. She wasn't even sure where that much had come from—some dusty vault in the recesses of her memory.

She screeched the strings a few times, stumbled over notes, and messed up the tempo so much trying to remember that it was impossible for anyone to actually join her. She felt heat flush her face and neck, but was surprised to find that, instead of feeling humiliation at being put on the spot and making an idiot out of herself, she found the experience to be remarkably freeing. These people weren't here to criticize her, and none of them were making rude remarks or gritting their teeth. They looked somewhat confused, but that couldn't really be helped.

She couldn't remember the entire song, and kind of fizzled off in an ending of erratic, helter-skelter notes. Then, stifling a giggle, she plunked out the last part of "Pop Goes the Weasel," which made all of the musicians erupt into laughter.

She shook her head and handed the viola back to its rightful owner. "I think you'd better take this back before I damage it permanently...or damage your eardrums permanently. One or the other." She shot Liron a teasing scowl. "Now that you've embarrassed me for the evening..."

He chuckled. "You told me you could play viola."

"I could...in high school. I'm a pianist!" Laughter echoed from everyone again and the warmth in Liron's eyes was going to be her undoing. She shook her head and put her hands on her hips. "I've done my part. Now, let me hear some real music."

Something else came to life within his eyes, something darker and much more dangerous to her heart. He slipped the guitar off and handed it to its owner, then reached for the viola again. He handed it back to Melody, who took it with bewilderment, then he went around behind her. "Try again."

He whispered it against her ear in a sinful caress of sound that sent shivers all the way down her spine and made her head spin. Her eyes fluttered closed while her breath left her. "Wh-what?" she stammered. "Liron, I don't remember anything else." Her protest sounded feeble even to her own ears.

"Don't play something you remember. Just play." He wrapped his fingers around her hand that held the viola.

She frowned. "How am I supposed to play randomly? I've never been any good at improvisation. Especially on an instrument I haven't played in—" She sucked her breath in sharply as he placed his hands on her shoulders, then drew them down her back in a way that made her shudder. He trailed one finger, just one, back up her spine, and ripples of sensual fire coursed throughout her body, creating notes in her mind no one should have been able to hear without the aid of some kind of black magic. Dark notes from the harmonic minor scale that somehow sounded so much more erotic than they ever had before, like she had been granted access to a new dimension of music that was forbidden.

Her eyes closed involuntarily and she let out a shuddering breath. His hand continued its journey along the arm that was holding onto the viola, and he gently guided it up to her shoulder. His other hand entangled in her hair and traced the length.

The notes in her mind exploded like some sort of grand symphonic composition and became so overwhelming that playing was almost a compulsion. She had to play them. She had to get them out of her mind and share them with anyone who would listen.

As if her body moved on its own, not unlike how she had felt when she'd played almost half of Liron's score without even looking at it, Melody positioned the bow over the strings on the viola and began to play what she heard in her mind. From somewhere deep inside the recesses of her memory, it all came back to her like she had played the viola only yesterday.

She lost herself within the dark, wonderful notes, lost herself in Liron's touch, and wanted to express the way he made her feel the only way she could at the moment—through the instrument in her hands.

If stumbling through "Russian Sailor's Dance" had been a freeing feeling simply because she was learning to embrace playing music again, this experience made her feel like she was flying. She had never before felt anything like the music that coursed through her body and mind while Liron continued to lazily drag his fingers up her spine, along her shoulders, and anywhere else he felt like touching.

She didn't know how long she played. It didn't matter. She didn't stop until he stopped infusing her with music, and that didn't stop until he took his hands off of her. Then, the notes faded and she was able to think clearly again. She opened her eyes and sucked in a deep breath while the other musicians applauded and cheered.

"How did you do that?" she murmured to Liron.

He placed his hands on her shoulders and squeezed gently, then placed his mouth to her ear. "It's what I do."

The caressing whisper of his voice made her woozy, and the strength left her body while a rush of wonderful notes coursed through her like electricity. Her fingers fumbled and she accidentally let go of the viola.

"Whoa!" the owner of the instrument shouted, leaping forward to catch it before it crashed to the ground. "Hey, maybe you want to seduce the human when she's *not* holding my viola?" His tone was good-natured, and he threw Liron a smirk.

Melody's cheeks burned and she leaned back against Liron, wanting to escape, and at the same time, wanting to be as close to him as possible. He pressed his lips tenderly to her temple and wrapped his arms around her waist. "You play magnificently," he said softly.

She turned in his arms so she could look up into his eyes. "Do you affect all humans that way? Does everyone hear music like that when you touch them?"

He reached up to touch her hair. "Only the ones who want to listen." He slowly dragged his fingers the length of her locks, causing lovely, tinkling sounds to echo in her mind. His smile was wicked and beautiful. "And only when I want someone to hear."

Melody closed her eyes and relished the effect he had on her. "I wish I could make you hear wonderful things when I touch you."

"Melody, don't you understand?" He was whispering in her ear again, turning her legs to jelly and her heart to putty in his hands. "Everything I share with you, all the notes and chords, are a direct result of what you cause me to hear. You inspire me so that I may, in turn, inspire you. It's the perfect balance we strive for between...."

He pulled back and let the sentence remain unformed. She frowned in curiosity at the slightly bashful expression on his face. "Between what?" she prodded.

He met her gaze and smiled shyly. "Between mates."

She wasn't entirely sure what it was her heart did in that moment, with the way his soft voice said those words while his blue eyes burned into hers with such sincerity and warmth. If she had to liken its actions to something, she would have to say it did something that felt kind of like "The Macarena," like it was dancing and gyrating in her chest. Whatever it was, it took her breath and made her ache for him so badly that she actually had lurid visions of ripping off his shirt right there in the middle of the square.

"Hey, Liron, are you still going to play with us?" one of the musicians called.

He didn't take his eyes off of her. "Do you still want me to?" he asked her. "Or would you like to go home?"

"Home?" A pain twinged through her heart at the thought of returning to her sterile living environment.

"I meant...my home." He stepped closer to her, close enough that she could feel the heat from his body.

She tossed around her options. She wanted to go anywhere with him right now. Anywhere where they could be alone and she could kiss him for real without someone, or something, interrupting them. But she also wanted to watch him play, experience his world, his culture and his life.

She placed her palms on his chest and smirked up at him playfully. "No worming your way out of it now, mister. Nice try."

He grinned and chuckled, then took her hands in his, kissed both of them, and winked at her while he walked around her and back over to the others. He took the guitar he had been holding before, slipped it back over his shoulder, and tuned it briefly before the man with the tribal drums called a three-count. They all launched into a Celtic-sounding song that seemed like it had been rehearsed a hundred times over.

Melody watched in rapt wonderment as every one of them seemed to be perfectly in sync with each other, even though she knew they were jamming and did not play together on a regular basis. She knew for a fact that Liron had not played with them before. He hadn't played anything in ages. The fact that they were all so fluid with one another amazed her, but then, maybe that was the way it was with muses.

If Liron could communicate such wonderful music to her through touch, and she knew that muses could contact humans through dreams and telepathy, she imagined their ability to connect and communicate with one another was that much greater.

She watched him play, watched how all of them became carried away with the music. The dancers started up again, followed by some of the fire jugglers who moved in time to the music to create more of a show.

It was impossible not to get caught up in the enchanted atmosphere, and given her love for music, Melody found it useless to remain stationary. Gypsy hooker costume aside, she threw her usual inhibitions to the wind and joined the others in dancing to the lively tune.

The music captivated and entranced her, and she found herself swept away by the carefree simplicity of it all. The other dancers welcomed her, laughed with her, and for the first time since her parents had died, she did not feel that burdening weight on her shoulders and heart. She felt light, happy, like her old self.

She linked arms with one of the other women and danced in a circle, kicking up her heels and spinning with abandon. She even found herself liking the way the gauzy skirt floated around her ankles.

She caught Liron's eye from where she was dancing, and the world seemed to fall away. The music dulled and her movements slowed. All she was aware of was the throbbing sound of her own heartbeat in her ears. The desire to dance suddenly dissipated as the blazing blue of his eyes held hers. They burned a trail down her body, and she took a step closer to him, drawn to his talent, his beauty, his touch, everything that made him who he was.

Almost simultaneously, he took the guitar from his shoulder and set it aside, then made up the distance between them with a couple strides. They stared into one another's eyes for a long, tormenting moment before he reached down and took her hand.

She didn't ask where he was taking her as he started to lead her out of the marketplace. She didn't care. He could have taken her to the freaking moon and she wouldn't have blinked twice. All she cared about was being with him, hearing his song. Nothing else in the world mattered to her besides the rapturous music she heard when he touched her. It was music that didn't hurt, didn't make her remember painful things. It soothed and healed. It scorched and burned through her body in an erotic, lurid flame. He was the greatest masterpiece she'd always wanted to create, but had never quite been able to hear all the notes of.

They traveled in silence out of the town and along the shoreline back toward Liron's home. His hand clutched hers with an urgency she felt also. As they approached the cliffs where the angry evening waves pounded against the rock with cacophonous vehemence, Liron tugged her off the main path and down to the beach. He led her close to the shore and to the base of the cliffs where they were out of danger of the waves but could still hear the thundering sound and taste the salt in the air.

He slowed enough to gently take Melody by the shoulders and guide her back against the rock. He searched her eyes for a brief moment before taking her face in his hands and crushing his lips to hers, releasing all the pent up frustration and tension he must have been feeling from their many near-kisses and subsequent interruptions.

Melody's fingers gripped the front of his shirt as electric fire sizzled through her veins, followed by a wave of sensual music. Not just notes, but an entire score. While his lips played over hers, she could hear and feel every instrument as if his mouth was conducting an orchestra in her body. She gasped at the sensations, and he took advantage of her surprise, sweeping his tongue past her lips to deepen the kiss and pull her further into the world of melodic bliss he created within her.

She groaned and drew closer to him, kissing him back with an abandon and wanton brazenness that she was unaccustomed to. The music he filled her with increased until she felt it pulsing throughout every nerve and vein with every beat of her heart. It was the soundtrack to the fervid dance their lips and tongues were engaged in, and the most powerful aphrodisiac Melody had ever experienced.

He pressed against her, trapping her between the rock and himself in a vise she never wanted to escape from. She drew her hands over his shoulders and down his back, caressing every sinuous line and taut muscle. He entangled his fingers in her hair and tugged gently, turning her face upward and exposing her throat. He tore his lips from hers and descended to her neck, trailing his tongue and teeth across her skin in a way that made hot shivers break out along every available surface of her body.

The music coiled within her, filling her until every one of her senses was overwhelmed. She felt deliriously hot, and her hands roamed over Liron's back, chest, and torso as if they had minds of their own. She wanted, needed, and *had to* touch him. It was a compulsion and a driving necessity.

When he brought his lips back to hers and claimed another kiss, her world exploded, imploded, and then shattered. Everything within her went inside, outside, and every direction, erupting into a strange release full of wonderful notes and magical sound. White-hot sensation flooded her, and she didn't realize she had cried out until Liron pulled back from her, withdrawing his music enough for her to be able to reclaim some sense.

She blinked slowly, trying to clear the fog from her mind.

Her lips felt deliciously swollen, and her nerves hummed with delight. She looked up at Liron, who had a soft, satisfied smile on his face, and her eyebrows drew together in question. "Did I just, like...scream?"

He chuckled softly and reached up to brush back her hair with a nod.

Heat flooded into her cheeks, and she buried her face against his shoulder. "Oh geez, how embarrassing." Although, she wasn't completely surprised. She knew music was powerful and that it could touch people on the deepest kind of level, but she had never figured it was physically possible to have some sort of near-orgasmic experience because of it. It wasn't strange that she had screamed because, well, it had been intense.

And fantastic.

"Don't be embarrassed," he purred, enveloping her in his embrace while he buried his hands in her hair. "I wanted you to scream. It let me know I was doing it right."

She pulled back to stare up into his face. "You mean you did that on purpose?"

His grin was wolfish. "Of course I did." He gave a lazy shrug with one shoulder. "The nice thing about being a muse is that there are ways to arouse someone besides physical stimulation." His eyes swept over her with a ravenous look that heated her blood all over again. "Not that I would be opposed to that."

He trailed his fingers down her bare arms and brought his hands to her exposed midsection. He rested his palms against her sides, stroking small circles across her skin with his thumbs. Melody closed her eyes at the warm, velvet contact.

"Humans are far too narrow-minded when it comes to intimacy," he continued. "Creativity can be just as stimulating as touch...if shared and experienced correctly."

She arched an eyebrow in a bland, teasing expression. "Well, I'm pretty sure you don't need any help in that department." She flushed again as she recalled the sensations. "I love music, desperately. It is and always has been my passion in life. But I never thought it could touch me...you know...like *that.*"

He chuckled again and trailed a row of sweet kisses along her jawline. "It is usually difficult for a human to feel a muse's influence that strongly. That makes you very special...that makes our connection very special. It is something two muse mates usually share. Two mates who have learned one another over time, who have adapted to each other and share the same vision." He shook his head and frowned thoughtfully. "I have never known of a human to have the same connection with a muse, and definitely not this quickly."

"Well, how many humans have been able to, how did you say it, traverse the continuum?"

He smiled and brought his palm up to cradle her cheek. "None that I know of. You are a rarity, Melody. A treasure I am tempted to keep for my own, even though I do not have that right."

The potency of his words, and the truth of them that she felt within her own heart, made her shiver. The frightening part of all of this was, the more time she spent with Liron, the more she shared with him and learned of his world, the more appealing the thought of letting him keep her seemed.

She didn't feel oppressed and despondent in this world full of life and creation. And the music she heard with him didn't hurt. Her heart did not feel that awful heaviness when she was resonating with his song. For the first time since that horrid day a year ago when that police officer had come to her door, she felt like she could take a full breath.

With a soft sigh, Melody took Liron's hands in her own. "You know, Liron, that option is starting to look more and more promising, so you'd better mean it when you say stuff like that to me."

Faint surprise registered over his features, and he studied her for a moment before he turned and led her over to a large log scattered amongst driftwood and seaweed. She sat and shivered as the ocean air chilled her exposed flesh. Belly dancing attire didn't offer much by way of warmth.

"I mean every word I say to you, Melody," Liron murmured as he sat down beside her and slipped his arm around her shoulders. He pulled her close to his body, sharing his warmth, and his wonderful scent invaded her nostrils. It was intoxicating, much like the rest of him. "Always." He all but whispered the word, and it took root deep inside of her. "I have lived more in this day with you than I have in many years. You have brought me more beauty in two days than I have ever known. For however you want me, in whatever role you choose to have me fill, for as long as you desire, I am yours."

His words didn't frighten her like they should have. It was illogical because she wasn't, by nature, a rash person. She thought things out before she did them. She weighed the pros and cons of situations before making decisions that could alter the course of her life—like thinking she might want to spend the rest of it in an alternate reality with a man who, by definition, was not human.

The rational part of her said she needed to go back home where she belonged. But did she belong there? What did she have to go back to, really? Everything she had loved was either gone or tarnished. There were ghosts everywhere she went of a life she could have had, but now never would. She felt like half a person in her world. She could be different in Liron's realm. She could start over, have new adventures and a new path. One that wasn't littered with remnants of a past full of heartache.

Besides, she was beginning to think that the rational part of her had taken a leave of absence.

She chewed on her bottom lip thoughtfully before turning her eyes up to Liron's captivating visage. "Those are heavy words, Liron. That isn't a light kind of commitment. What if I decide to take you up on it?"

It was a challenge she feared the answer to. After all, he had had his heart ripped out, and he barely knew her. Words were lovely when coming from such beautiful lips as his, but he was still a man. And in the heat of the moment, men said things that—

All of her thoughts ceased abruptly as he brought those beautiful lips down on hers again. Music barraged her, assaulted her, forced its way into her where it flowed the blazing hot path of her blood to her heart. She felt him in that music. Felt his gentleness and his compassion, felt the essence of him in her soul while she tasted it on his tongue. She felt the truth of his words, and the resolve of his commitment. He would be hers if she asked him to be.

The question she had to ask herself was did she want him to be? Or a better question—did she have the courage to alter her entire life to be his in return?

Chapter Eleven

"Liron, can I ask you a weird question?"

He looked over at her, huddled in front of the fireplace, wrapped up in a blanket. She looked so comfortable, so at home in his world. He poured them each a glass of red wine and returned to his own chair, offering her one of the glasses. "You can ask me anything."

She smiled and took a sip. She gazed into the flames for a moment, then heaved a resigned-sounding sigh. "How do muses mate?" He frowned at her and color crept into her cheeks as she shook her head. "Wait, that came out wrong."

He chuckled and sipped his own drink, waiting for her to continue.

"I mean, is it like in my world? When you get married? With a big ceremony and a marriage license and such?"

"Generally, arranged marriages are quite a big deal. They are supposed to be ideal matches, so we have grand parties and showy spectacles." He rolled his eyes.

She giggled. "Was your wedding like that?"

"Unfortunately." He sighed and glanced over at her. "I'm a generally quiet person. I like my privacy and kind of wanted to keep my love affair, or lack thereof, intimate and personal. Elizabeth wanted the big hurrah, though. I actually think she was happier planning that behemoth of a party than she was one day with me."

"Are all of your marriages arranged?"

He shook his head. "No, it's a tradition that goes back longer than I know the history of. It's a family's choice whether or not they wish to arrange a marriage for their children. Many muses marry for love and love alone. In those cases, the ceremony is not nearly as enormous. And we do not require a license to marry. In the simplest of ceremonies, all a couple need do is stand before two witnesses and pledge their vow to one other. That is considered legal and binding."

He glanced over at her as she seemed to turn this over in her mind and quietly sip her wine.

"You say there have never been any humans who have been able to come to this realm before?" she finally asked.

He shrugged. "I'm not sure. I have never heard of any personally, but that does not mean there never has been. I imagine if it is possible for you, it could be possible for others...if the connection was strong enough."

"Like the connection I have with you," she assumed, meeting his gaze. "The one we share through your music." At his nod, she pulled her bottom lip between her teeth and chewed on it until he was sure she was going to gnaw it off. "Do you think it's possible for a human to stay in this realm?"

"I don't see why not." He frowned in thought, set his glass down and rose from the chair. He went to kneel in front of her so he could look up into her eyes. "Why the interest?" He quirked an eyebrow and offered a playful smile. "All this talk of marriage ceremonies and humans remaining in the muse realm.... You plan on staying a while?" He reached up to tuck back an errant strand of her golden hair. "Plan on making me your mate?"

He meant only to tease her, but she met his gaze boldly, with determined focus and said, "And if I am?"

His heart tumbled over itself several times to the point that it robbed him of his ability to draw in a breath. His eyes widened and he stared at her, trying to gauge if she was serious or only playing with him. When she didn't crack a smile or start laughing, his breath came out in a whoosh and he shook his head. "Melody, that option sounds promising, so you had better mean it when you say things like that to me," he murmured, paraphrasing her words from earlier.

A warm, soft smile split her lips, and she reached out to thread her fingers through his hair and trail them down the length of the strands. "I mean every word I say to you," she said. "Always."

His heart started to beat double-time, and he closed his eyes as he let her words fill up every dark, lonely space inside him with radiant hope. What would it be like to be with someone who actually desired him? Who set him on fire every time he looked at her and accepted his music into herself like it belonged there and she craved it? Who looked at him with warmth and affection in the depths of her eyes instead of cold apathy? He had long ago stopped imagining that he would ever have such a thing. Could it be possible that Melody—this amazing woman who felt him across the continuum, traveled to his world at will, who made him hear symphonies unlike anything he had ever experienced—could really want to give him the greatest gift in existence—her love?

He sucked in a slow breath to calm his erratic and overwhelming emotions and looked up at her again. "Melody, to be chosen by one such as you to be your mate…." He shook his head and looked down, feeling unworthy even as he felt flattered. "I would be humbled and honored." He moved to sit cross-legged on the floor in front of her chair, taking her hand in both of his and caressing the softness of her skin, needing to touch her, to feel that she was real and not some deluded fantasy. "But you need to realize the weight of that kind of commitment. Time passes slowly in this dimension. If you were to choose to remain here with me, it would be for a very long time." He hated putting any sort of doubt in her mind when everything inside of his was screaming to capitalize on what she was saying. But he cared for and respected her too much to take advantage of her feelings just because he was lonely and hopelessly lost to her. She needed to understand what she was saying before she made a decision she could end up regretting.

To his surprise, she set her wine glass down and moved out of the chair. She sat in his lap, straddling his waist and wrapping her long legs around his hips in a way that almost caused him to spontaneously combust. He sucked his breath in and placed his hands on her hips as she shifted her weight in order to sit comfortably, resulting in her being even more intimately pressed against him. "What, are you trying to kill me?" he teased, his voice coming out gruffer than he'd ever heard himself sound.

Her satisfied giggle almost undid him, and as she wrapped her arms around his neck and buried her delicate hands in his hair, he groaned and let his forehead fall onto her shoulder helplessly. He was so starved for affection, his body had no idea how to react to it, how to process the burning ache she created within him.

"If I told you I was honestly, seriously considering it, would you...I mean...." Her words trailed off, and he looked up to see that she had averted her gaze to the ground. Her bold bravado had slipped; she seemed lost and confused. She flushed and shook her head. "What am I saying?"

He smiled softly and cupped her cheek in his palm. "What *are* you saying?"

She fixed him with a sidelong glance and snorted. "I'm not sure, but it sounded an awful lot like I was going to propose to you, didn't it?" Her face turned a deeper shade of crimson and he chuckled.

He pushed her hair back, exposing her neck, and he tilted her chin sideways so he could access it with his lips. He trailed soft kisses down her jaw and along the column of her throat, drawing a soft sigh from her. He felt the hammering of her pulse and was delighted that he could affect her the same way she seemed to affect him. He swirled his tongue along that pulse and smiled at her sharp intake of breath.

"Whatever you decide, I will support you," he whispered between kisses. "If you wish to choose me, and remain in this world, you will make me the happiest man in any dimension. But if you decide that you need to return to your world, I will find a way to follow you there...and I'll be your dutiful stalker." Her laughter was more musical to him than any instrument he had ever heard. Her arms tightened around his neck, pulling him closer, and he buried his face against her shoulder.

"Would you really do that, Liron?" she asked after a few moments, pulling back so that she could look into his eyes. "Follow me to my world?"

He searched her beautiful blue depths and lost himself there. "You have brought me life again," he murmured. "You have brought me laughter and light. You have brought me music again. I would follow you anywhere."

So many emotions reflected in her eyes that he couldn't put a label on all of them. She nestled in his arms, snuggled against him with so much warmth and so much trust. His heart ached at the affection she showed him, the acceptance and the *want* of him. For so long he had wondered what it would feel like to be wanted. He had never imagined it would be so all-consuming, so life-altering. He had never imagined that something as simple as feeling wanted would end up being not simple at all, or that he would be ready to drop his whole world, everything he had ever known, just to be near one woman.

But he would.

Because there was no way he could go without the song she brought to life within him. Not now that he had heard it.

A loud knocking and the incessant ringing of a bell ripped him out of his precious moment with Melody. She lifted her head with a frown and looked at him. "You expecting someone?" she queried.

He shook his head and his heart fell as he glanced past her shoulder to the far side of his room. "That's not for me, my lovely." He pointed over to where her home had manifested itself across his floor and walls.

She glanced over her shoulder and her surprise was more than apparent. She pushed herself off his lap and into a standing position, then went over toward the portal into her world.

"Melody? Melody, are you in there?" A distinct, feminine voice could be heard while the bell continued to ring.

Liron arched an eyebrow. "Friend of yours?"

She looked back at him with shock etched into her features. She pointed to the daylight streaming through her window. "How long have I been here?"

"Melody!" The woman hollered again, as if she'd heard the conversation. "Where are you? I haven't heard from you in four days!"

Melody started. "Four days?" she practically screeched. "Oh my gosh, I'm gonna get fired!" She spun and held her hands out to him, which he immediately took. Regret washed over her features. "Liron, I have to go back for a little bit, just to make sure everyone knows I'm okay. No one knew I was going anywhere. They're going to be worried. And I probably lost my job."

He brought her fingers to his lips and kissed them tenderly. "Of course."

She stepped closer to him and caressed the length of his hair. "I'll come back as soon as I can, okay?"

He smiled, even though his heart ached at the thought of

her leaving for any amount of time. "I'll be here."

She smiled at him and her eyes filled with warmth. "Promise?"

He lowered his lips to hers and kissed her slowly, cherishing the petal-softness of her perfect mouth. He nuzzled his nose against hers when he pulled away. "Always."

"Melody!" *Ringringringringring!* Her friend was extremely persistent.

She stepped out of his embrace and started toward the doorway to her world. She stopped when she reached the threshold and looked back at him. She smiled and blew him a kiss that pierced his heart. Then, she was gone.

He tried to ignore the horrible fear that, this time, she would not be able to return to him. She had the music score, which was the key to her ability to travel. And besides, even if she was unable to reach him, somehow, he would find a way to get to the human world. He would not be parted from her now that he had found her. She was his life song. And as long as she wished it, he would move heaven and earth to be by her side.

Melody wasted no time in heading toward the door once she was back in her world. By the sound of it, Nikki was about to have a nervous breakdown. And she couldn't really blame her, in all reality. The fact that she had actually been gone for four days was hard for her to wrap her mind around. By her calculations, she had only been with Liron for maybe three quarters of a day. The fact that time went so much faster in her world was something she couldn't quite get used to.

She opened the door, revealing Nikki looking first frantic, then aggravated. "Melody!" she all but screamed. "Where have you been? I've been worried sick!" She yanked the screen door open and barreled in without waiting for an invitation. "I called your cell phone about a hundred times. Where were you that you couldn't call me—?" She stopped short as she noticed Melody's attire and her eyebrow rose in perplexed curiosity. "What in the world are you wearing?"

"Uh...." She searched for words. "It's my new hobby. Belly dancing."

"Belly dancing." Nikki sounded about as convinced as a parent who had just caught their child doing something questionable. She folded her arms. "And this took up so much of your time that you couldn't bother to call back your best friend who thought you were dead somewhere?" She was back to screaming again. "I went by your work and they said they hadn't heard from you either! It's not like you to no call, no show, Mel. What is going on?"

"I went out of town." It wasn't really a lie. She *had* gone out of town.

Nikki blinked in bewilderment. "You went out of town? On a whim? Where did you go?"

"To the coast," she replied quickly, then tried to hide the flush that crept into her cheeks at her memory of kissing Liron at the cliffs.

Nikki stared at her for several long moments, as if trying to assess whether or not Melody had finally lost her mind. Then, she cocked her head to the side and her eyes narrowed like she was picking up on something she was trying to figure out. Slowly, her eyes widened and she sucked in a breath. "Oh my gosh, you met someone." It was a statement of fact, not a question, and Melody's face betrayed her by blushing worse. "You *did!*" Nikki screeched. "You have to tell me!" She snatched Melody's wrist and hauled her down to sit next to her on the couch. "First, tell me why you decided to go to the coast anyway."

"Uh...." She didn't want to lie to her friend, but how was she supposed to explain that she had somehow defied the laws of physics and traveled to another dimension? Or that the man she had met was not really a man by human standards, but a who-knew-how-old muse whose touch made her hear and feel music? Or that she was seriously contemplating the idea of staying in that dimension permanently and making said muse her mate when she really hadn't known him for longer than a couple days? She could barely comprehend all of that on her own. How did she expect Nikki to?

So she decided to tell the closest thing to the truth that she could without sounding like a lunatic. "Actually, I did some research on that music score and managed to find out where a...relative of the composer lived. I decided to track him down on a whim." *Close enough.*

Nikki raised an eyebrow. "Like a friggin' stalker? Dang, Mel. Did you hide in his bushes too?"

Melody laughed and swatted her friend on the arm. "No...I dunno. I needed to get away for a while, you know? So I just decided to go."

"And you found this dude?"

Melody's cheeks turned hot again, and she wanted to smack herself. What was she? Thirteen? "Yeah, I found him." Her voice sounded so breathy it was ridiculous.

"And?" Nikki was practically bouncing in place.

Melody giggled. "He's a musician too."

Nikki snorted with a look that said, *no duh*. "Well, of course."

"We talked about music a lot, played some...." Shivers worked along her spine at the recollection of the music his touch infused her with. She glanced up at Nikki, who was looking at her with a knowing smirk and a sparkle in her eyes.

"Are you going to see him again?"

Melody bit her bottom lip. "Yes, I would like to. As soon as possible."

Nikki raised both of her eyebrows in surprise. "Shoot, you have it bad, girl! You need to tell me absolutely everything, pronto. Let's go grab some lunch."

"Okay, lemme put on something a little more presentable, huh?" She stood and headed to her bedroom. In truth, she really wanted to take a hot shower. She still felt groady from the hog slop incident.

"Mel?"

She turned to look at Nikki over her shoulder.

Nikki gave her a look full of mischief. "He's super hot, isn't he?"

Melody felt something melt inside of her, and she nodded dreamily. "Oh yeah."

Chapter Twelve

Melody returned home from lunch with Nikki feeling light-hearted and happy. She had divulged as much as would make sense about Liron, and Nikki's positive personality had been contagious. True, she didn't know that Melody was considering going and living in an alternate universe, but that aside, Nikki had given her the green light on the whole thing. Melody figured her friend was probably just happy to see her doing something other than moping around like a misplaced zombie.

Setting her purse and keys down, Melody went over to her answering machine and checked for messages. There were about a hundred from Nikki, frantically wondering where she had vanished to, and about a hundred more from Rob. She rolled her eyes and deleted her way through those as quickly as possible. She had no desire to deal with him at the moment. Now that she thought about it, she had no idea why she had ever given him the time of day in the first place. Just because he was a distraction, she guessed. He took her mind off of her pain for half a second and filled it with annoyance instead. Yeah, that was healthy.

She smirked and her heart did acrobatics at the recollection of Liron's musical touch and kisses. She much preferred his kind of distraction. And after being inundated with music for the past whoever-actually-knew-how-long, she didn't understand how she could have ever thought she could live without it in her life. What a coward she had been.

In harmony with her wandering thoughts, a message came from the music director of the orchestra she had once been part of. He told her that he was guest conducting a different orchestra at a large music festival nearby and wanted to invite her.

Melody glanced at the calendar. The event was tonight. Her first reaction was to avoid it at all costs, but then something inside of her made her think twice. There would be no harm in going to watch an old friend, and there was no reason for her to be afraid of music anymore. It lived and breathed within her; she could not escape it, and she would be doing a disservice to herself and her parents' memory if she tried.

She looked at the clock, then headed back to her bedroom. She had about three hours before the festival began. She'd find something presentable to wear and make an appearance.

As she walked down the hall, she glanced at Liron's music and smiled to herself. She was anxious to get back to him, but it could wait until after the festival. She also had some business to attend to before she headed back to Liron's world. Such as calling her job to ask when she could pick up her last paycheck, since even if they let her, she would not be returning. Whether she decided to stay in Liron's world or not, she would not continue to work at a dead-end job she abhorred when she could be doing something else she loved.

She couldn't hide from her passion anymore. Music found her regardless of where she went or how she tried to avoid it. It found her and called to her.

And she wanted to answer.

She felt beautiful as she took her seat in the balcony at the theatre. She had dressed to kill, knowing that, after she returned home from the concert, she would be going back to Liron, and she wanted to knock his socks off. She was dressed in a navy blue dress that came to her knees with a V-neck that showed more than its fair share of cleavage. At her throat, she wore a silver and sapphire necklace her mother had given her when she'd graduated from Juilliard, and she had her blonde waves flowing free with only the sides pinned back with silver clips. She knew Liron liked to bury his fingers in it, so she figured she would make it easier for him to do just that.

She didn't feel as apprehensive as she had imagined she would as she sat through the first half of the show. The music was wonderful, and her anxiety diminished to the point that she actually found herself wrapped up in and enjoying the pieces as she once had, before the accident.

She settled in for the second half of the show as the lights dimmed and the curtain raised again, delighting in how Liron's influence had taken so much of the pain out of her life that had been associated with music. She had never really *wanted* to stop playing, to stop loving it. Just, after the accident, she hadn't been able to face it. Not when all of it held so many memories of her once-happy family and life.

Her friends had given her the "if you fall off the horse" speech so many different ways she couldn't see straight, and she'd known the truth of their words in her heart, but she just hadn't been able to embrace music the way she once had. It felt like it no longer had a place after her parents were gone. Even though she knew all of that reasoning had been illogical and only her grief talking, that's how she'd felt all the same.

Liron had changed all of that. Liron *was* music. Every elegant move of his body, every tender touch, everything that made him who he was. All of him was made of music. And she hadn't realized how much her soul still craved it, how empty she was without it, until he'd taken her in his arms and erased her pain with the gentleness of his song.

Melody sat back in her chair with a contented sigh as the music began, but the contentment was replaced by horrendous panic. At the first few notes, her heart dropped out of her chest and fell into an empty void, the ache within her so strong and instant that it stole her breath.

The haunting opening of "Adagio in G Minor" weaved its way through the theatre and, against her will, images of her parents filled her mind on the last day she had seen them, followed by images of their heart-wrenching funeral. She squeezed her eyes shut as the pain increased to something almost tangible. It was like someone had ripped open a still-tender wound and poured acid in it.

She tried to sit there and breathe it out, but the piece was long, and she was being constantly flooded by images of her happy-go-lucky, laughing father, her gentle mother, the three of them all playing their instruments together in a joyous kind of ruckus, then of the somber, tormenting melancholy of their caskets surrounded by flowers while the orchestra played this song in memoriam. And she stood all alone. Because regardless of the continued caring words and embraces, that was exactly what she had been. And that's what she still was. In this world anyway.

She had to get out of there. If she stayed one more minute, she was going to suffocate.

Propelling herself out of the chair with not as much dignity as she would have liked, she fled from the theatre. Her chest felt like someone was squeezing it in a vise, and she couldn't take a decent breath. She ran down the stairs and out the front door, finally managing to wheeze in a painful gasp of air when she got into her car and slammed the door. It was only then that she realized she had tears streaming down her face.

She touched them, stunned, because she had not been able to release tears since her parents had died. She had felt them sting, but they had never spilled over. They felt like they were burning as they fell.

Turning her car on and pulling out of the parking lot, she let them run without bothering to wipe them away. There was something morbidly therapeutic about the feel of them trailing down her cheeks.

When she reached her house, she pulled into the driveway, turned off the engine, and just sat there, crying softly. She finally wiped her eyes, but more tears replaced them as memories of her parents barraged her until her already broken heart felt like it was shattering all over again.

A sudden knock on her window made her scream and she jumped, looking up to see Rob peering curiously in at her. She rolled the window down and scowled at him. "You scared the freaking crap out of me!" she all but shouted.

"Sorry. What are you just sitting in the car for?" His gaze roamed over her face for a second before he frowned. "Have you been crying?"

She rolled her eyes and shoved her door open. *Brilliant assessment.*

"What happened?" he prodded as she climbed out.

"Nothing," she muttered. "I don't want to talk about it. And why were you lurking like a freaking creepy stalker?"

He ignored her. "Well, where were you? More importantly, where have you *been*? I thought you were avoiding me or something."

Gee, what would give you that impression? "I was away," she answered vaguely.

He made a rude noise in his throat. "Nice. Thanks for telling me."

"I wasn't aware that I needed a permission slip."

He heaved a sigh, but didn't acknowledge her sarcasm. "Well, now that you're back, maybe we could set up a date," he said as he followed her up to her front door. "You still owe me a dinner."

I don't owe you anything, you insensitive jackass. "Yeah, maybe. I don't know. I'm not really thinking straight right now. I'll get back to you."

He grabbed her elbow as she unlocked her door and tried to make her escape. "Mel, what in the world happened? Whatever it is, it can't be that bad."

Her spine went rigid at both his touch and his flip attitude. She fixed him with a dark look. "Not that bad?"

"Yeah," he said with a shrug and a snort. "Not worth all the female drama anyway." He stuffed his hands in his pockets and dared to smile.

The douchebag actually smiled.

Like it was all just a freaking joke.

Anger surged over the top of her sorrow, and she planted her palm on his chest, pushing him back down the porch steps. "Well, I'm sorry that the death of my parents is so insignificant to you, but I'm pretty sure you can't even relate to something of that magnitude since the only thing you've ever lost that was remotely important to you was your favorite pair of sunglasses when they fell off of your empty head while you were in your fishing boat. By all means, remove yourself from my 'female drama.' I'm more than okay with that since every time I see you lately, I imagine ripping off various parts of your body and beating you senseless with them. Get off my property and get away from me. I can't even begin to deal with you right now. All I want to do is play my piano, and all you're succeeding in doing is pissing me off!"

She left him standing there and all but took the door off the hinges trying to seek refuge within her home. She slammed it behind her, and the tears started again as soon as she knew she was alone. Only, this time, it was less quiet grief and more hysterical sobs.

She felt lost and out of control. The pain was all-consuming, choking her and making rational thought impossible.

She went to her piano and sat down, not bothering with anything in her house. She didn't want to be there. She wanted to be in Liron's arms. It was the only place she felt contentment. And he was the only person who could offer her solace and sanity.

It was difficult to play the notes with the tears gushing out of her eyes and obscuring her vision, and it was hard to concentrate when her mind was nothing but a muddled mess, but somehow, she managed to blunder through Liron's score. And maybe because her loneliness was so great, the emotion that seemed to be the driving force of the piece of music, it didn't take as long for the gateway to open.

She felt the shift in the room temperature and the way the sounds resonated around her, and she stopped playing abruptly. She looked over her shoulder to see Liron's living room beckoning her. The fire was smoldering in the fireplace with only enough light coming from the embers to make everything look eerie. Was it really only later in the same night that she had left? When it had been a whole day in her world?

Who cared? It didn't matter. Time, the laws of physics, the universe, nature—none of it meant jack squat to her at the moment. All that mattered was that she could escape this hellhole her life in the human world had become.

Crossing over into Liron's room, she didn't bother to call out, didn't bother to say anything. She merely went over to the fireplace, sat down in front of it, pulled her knees to her chest and sobbed like a lost little girl. She felt colder, darker, and more alone than she had since the day she'd watched her parents' caskets lowered into the ground.

"Melody?"

His voice made shudders course through her body, and she looked up into his blue eyes, full of concern and sincere compassion. It was the final straw. She collapsed into his arms, burying her face in his chest and crying dry, wracking sobs that robbed her of breath.

His arms enveloped her, held her close, and his fingers

buried in her hair as he pressed soft kisses to the top of her head. "Lovely, what happened?" he whispered.

"Th-they're *gone!*" she cried, as if that would explain everything.

Somehow, it seemed to do exactly that. He didn't ask her anything else, just lifted her effortlessly into his arms and carried her out of the room.

She clung to him, to his strength, solidity, and his warmth as he carried her down the staircase to his bedroom. He set her on the edge of his bed and bent to take off her shoes. Then, skimming his fingers up her calves in the process, he stood and gently eased her down so she was lying on her side. She curled her knees up and shivered.

Liron went around to the other side of the bed and pulled a blanket over her. He retreated for a moment to build a fire in the hearth in his room, then climbed onto the bed beside her and pulled her into his soothing embrace.

"I'm sorry for just showing up in the middle of the night," she murmured.

"Shhh." He brushed his lips across her hair and pulled her tighter. "Don't ever apologize for coming to me. You are welcome here forever and always."

She squeezed her eyes shut as a few more rogue tears escaped and she nestled against him, turning in his arms so she could bury her face against his shirt, breathe in his scent, and listen to the rhythm of his heartbeat. She sniffled, her torrential emotions abating to dismal sadness. "I went to see a friend of mine conduct for a music festival tonight," she said. "I was fine until they played the song that was played at my parents' funeral." He smoothed her hair back and she sighed. "It's a beautiful piece. It was their favorite, but I can't handle hearing it. It's like it rips my heart open all over again." He pressed gentle kisses to her forehead and face, letting her speak, but showing her he was there, and listening. "I don't know if the pain will ever go away."

"Of course it won't." His voice was tender, melodic and wonderful. "They were your parents, Melody. You loved them, and you miss them. The pain and sorrow of missing them is never going to go away, and you shouldn't expect it to."

Grief squeezed her chest again and she chewed on her bottom lip. "But everyone always says, 'time heals' and blah

blah blah. It's been a year and it still hurts like it happened yesterday."

"The pain will lessen over time, and you will learn to accept the ache of it, to live with it, but I would never expect you to get over it. The loss is too great."

She sniffed again. "I think everyone else thinks I should get over it. I don't know how they could if they were in my position."

"They care about you. They don't want to see you hurt, but sometimes humans lack the ability to formulate words in a way that is productive." He sighed and rolled onto his back, tugging her over on top of him so she was lying with her body flush against his. He held her close, and she snuggled against his chest.

They lay there in silence for several long moments and, slowly, his comforting presence started to replace the cold emptiness that had taken over her. He wasn't using his talent to its full extent. There were no symphonies in her mind, only the softest sounds of nature as he ran his fingers in long strokes through her hair. She marveled over how well he knew her in such a short time. He knew she wouldn't be able to handle the orchestral sensation at the moment, but that music, even in its most natural setting—the wind in the treetops, crickets on a summer night—was the one thing that could calm her. That and his persistent, kind touch.

The dark, gaping hole she had sworn was in her heart an hour ago began to be filled with Liron's tender light, and she heaved a sigh as the coiled tension within her slipped away. "Liron," she whispered.

"Yes, lovely."

She smiled at his term of endearment and closed her eyes as she listened to the steady beat of his beautiful heart. The words came easily to her now. So did the choice. "I want to stay in this world...with you."

His hands in her hair stilled for a second before he shifted them so that she was on her side, cradled in his arms, and he could look down at her. His brow was furrowed and his eyes mirrored mild surprise. "Melody...."

She let out a little, irritated sigh. "Liron, I'm not out of my mind, okay? So don't look at me like that. I'm a big girl, capable of making big girl choices. This is not my grief talk-

ing. I'm not running from anything. I was seriously considering this before tonight, and all of the stuff that happened just
solidified my decision." She ran her palm up his chest, feeling
the lines of muscle beneath his shirt, and desperately wanted
to see and touch those lines without the fabric in the way.

She studied his expression and a smidgen of uneasy
doubt crept into her. "Oh...unless...." She averted her gaze,
feeling stupid and presumptuous. "Unless you don't want—"

He cut off her words with a tender kiss to her lips that
took her breath away and inflamed her even as it soothed
and comforted. "Melody, I told you, I am yours. Whatever
you decide. I just don't want you to make a hasty decision
that you will later regret."

The care and compassion reflected in his eyes made her
heart flutter, and she pressed closer to him. "My world
doesn't offer me anything anymore, Liron," she murmured.
She closed her eyes as he held her and his fingers drew patterns across her back. "When I'm here, I don't feel that suffocating emptiness that I feel when I'm in my world. Your
world is full of life and beauty, of music and art and creation.
And...you."

A strange expression crossed his face. Something that
looked like it started out as joy, but was chased away by
worry. His hands on her back stilled and he looked away.
"And...you're certain that you...want me? Choosing me means
staying here, with me, for a very long time. You could get
tired of it all after a while."

His uncertainty tugged at her heart, and she pushed herself up into a sitting position so she could look at him fully.
Her intention had been to boldly set the record straight, but
her bravery fizzled and she looked down at her lap while she
played with her fingers. All of this was so foreign to her. She
felt so sure of her feelings in one moment, but then doubt
crept in. Doubt caused by what she'd been taught was "rational" her whole life. And nothing about Liron or inter-
dimensional travel came anywhere near "rational."

"Is it strange that...?" She cleared her throat and tried
again. "Is it strange that you can love someone so quickly?"

He sat up with a start and was in front of her before she
could even blink. There was so much intensity radiating from
his blue eyes it made her shiver. He took her gently by the

shoulders, and the notes that filled her mind were disjointed and seemed unintentional, chaotic, like several musicians had knocked over all their equipment. It tugged a smile from her lips, and she reached out to smooth his silky hair.

"What did you just say?" he whispered.

She sighed and continued to study the texture of his hair between her fingers. She gave a little self-conscious shrug, feeling like a naive teenager telling a boy she liked him for the first time. If her emotions got any more out of whack tonight... She'd never felt so many across-the-board things in one night in her life.

"Melody..." He took her face between his hands, and she closed her eyes. His palms were warm and velvet soft. His voice mirrored his touch perfectly. "Don't feel embarrassed. I need to hear what you said again. Please..." He rested his forehead against hers.

"It doesn't make sense, but...you feel right to me, Liron. You fit. You fill the empty place inside of me. I thought music was the only thing that could touch me so profoundly. It has always been my love, my anchor, my passion. How can I not love you the same way? You *are* music. Is that strange? That I have felt so connected to you from the moment I played your music? That I feel like we just make sense somehow?"

He shook his head. "No, it's not strange. That is the way of things in my realm. Muses are much more emotional creatures. We are ruled by passion and feelings much more than logic, the way humans are taught. From the moment you came wandering into my home, my heart has been tied to you. It was instantaneous. You are very easy to love."

Tears filled her eyes, but they had a different origin than her volatile ones from earlier. These were born of her heart feeling so safe and so full in that moment, so wrapped in wonderful warmth that she couldn't contain them. And it seemed that, now that they had let loose, they were going to come out at every given moment.

Liron touched her tears with his fingertips, then leaned in to kiss them away. She shivered and sniffed, then reached up to wipe at the remaining ones. "You know, I haven't cried since my parents died?"

He frowned. "No?"

She shook her head. "I couldn't. I don't know why. Tonight, they just...came out of nowhere. My emotions were so strong, I couldn't help it." She analyzed herself for a moment, and realized that she didn't feel quite as hollow as she had before. Her heart still ached at the absence of her loved ones, but it wasn't so overwhelming that it threatened to consume her. "It's weird, but...I feel a little better."

He nodded. "That makes sense. You finally released all of that pain."

She looked up into his eyes, finding the compassion and understanding there the most desirable things she'd ever seen. Her heart gave a little sigh of surrender. "I really do think I'm falling in love with you," she murmured. "Or, maybe, I already have fallen. I'm not sure."

He closed his eyes and an expression of serene bliss passed over his features. "There is no way for me to describe how hearing those words from you makes me feel," he said softly. "I only know one way to express it to you."

She smiled and cupped his strong jaw in her palm. "Show me."

Chapter Thirteen

Liron was so hopelessly lost to this woman.

His fingers flew over the piano keys, producing joyful yet sensual sounds that perfectly portrayed the feelings Melody ignited within him. She was the light streaming back into his world, touching all the dismal places Elizabeth and her treachery had left behind. She was *his* muse, awakening music within him like he had never heard or felt before.

He didn't have to think about the notes he played, didn't have to open his eyes to look at the keys. The music flowed through him freely, and he basked in the rapture of it.

It had been so long since he'd heard such rich melodies. She brought the most amazing music to him, along with the most amazing light and beauty. She made every corner of his previous dreary existence radiant.

His fingers faltered on the keys as he felt her hands stroke through his hair. He stilled his playing and sighed, smiling at how intimate and comfortable her touch was.

"This is how I affect you?" she murmured. "This music?" Her breath against his ear made his body ache with the need to touch and kiss her.

"It's the closest thing," he answered. "But even the music cannot do the feelings justice." He leaned back against her, and she wrapped her arms around his shoulders.

"Keep playing," she said.

He grinned. "How do you expect me to do that when you're distracting me the way you are?"

She laughed softly and moved around to sit beside him on the piano bench. His eyes took in her navy blue dress that hugged her curves in all the right places and gave him the most marvelous view of her chest. Because of her emotional state when she'd arrived, he had not noticed the lovely garment before now. His heart leaped and rolled, and he smiled.

"That is an extraordinary dress, Melody."

The grin she dazzled him with let him know that she had originally hoped to receive that reaction, despite the way her evening had turned out.

She glanced deliberately at the piano keys. "Play," she demanded.

He leaned over and feathered several soft kisses along her jaw. "What would you like?" he whispered, delighting in the shiver he felt work through her.

"Play what this sounds like." She turned her head to capture his lips with hers. The kiss was gentle, but tinged with something much more intense. It made him recall the kisses they'd shared down by the cliffs, and his body came alive with fire and aching hunger.

He deepened the kiss, taking control and wanting to taste her beauty the same way he heard it and felt it. He wanted all of his senses filled with Melody until there was nothing else. He'd never wanted a woman more than he wanted this one. It was all-consuming, drowning out even his passion and love for music. She was a symphony all in her own, and the only song he ever wanted to hear for the rest of his days.

She laughed softly against his lips, but her voice came out breathy. "You're supposed to be playing the piano, not playing with my mouth," she teased.

A low growl was torn from his throat, and he reached down to grasp her around the waist. "You want to know what your kiss sounds like?" She squeaked in surprise and wrapped her arms around his neck as he lifted her off of the piano bench and set her down on top of the keys. The result was a cacophonous menagerie of everything at once.

The row of keys was not wide enough for her to stay seated on and she slid down until her feet touched the floor, creating more disjointed, random sound. He kept her there, leaning back against the keys, and he stared down into her eyes, feeling primal and out of control. He was, by nature, a gentle person. But this woman was invading him in such a way that all he wanted to do was possess her, claim her, make her his for all time. The music in his mind was jumbled and confusing. It was so much more than he'd ever felt before. Was this how it was supposed to be? Had he found his perfect inspiration in a human woman who'd accidentally wandered into his life?

She reached up to thread her fingers through his hair and his lips descended onto hers again. He ravaged her mouth, pushing her back against the piano keys until she was forced to arch her back because of the angle. He slipped his arm around her lower back and pulled her up against him, tearing his lips away from hers and trailing deliberate, smoldering kisses down the column of her throat.

She sighed and let her head fall back as he nibbled and teased her skin, following the low cut line of her dress. He felt her heart thundering, and he reached up to unclasp and remove her necklace, then trailed his tongue lazily across one side of her collarbone and back up her neck to nip her earlobe. He delved his fingers into her thick, lustrous hair and played his lips along her jaw a little longer before finding her mouth again.

He tried to get his wildly spinning mind under control enough to send the music dancing through her as he had done before. It was difficult to concentrate when everything in him was wrapped up in her, but he managed to regain some semblance of balance and sent some notes drifting and cavorting through her, just enough to make her tremble.

It worked. She groaned softly and bit down on his bottom lip. He gave a quiet chuckle, delighting in the effect his talent had on her. She made him feel so sexy, so wanted, so alive.

Her fingers found their way beneath his shirt and trailed up his sides, leaving lines of scorching fire in their wake. She drew her nails lightly back down and he shivered.

"Liron." His name left her lips in the sultriest breath of sound. "Do you really think I could be your mate?"

"There is no one in this world or any other better suited to me than you," he murmured while moving his lips to her neck again.

"I want to stay here," she whispered.

"I want that as well."

"I want to always stay here. I want to be yours." He slowly drew his fingers up her bare arm in a music-infused caress. She shuddered and her hands came up to grip his shoulders. She pushed him back gently, enough for her to stand up straight, and broke just enough of the spell to be taken seriously. "I mean it. I want to be yours."

He nodded, frowning in slight confusion. "I've never denied you, Melody. As long as you want to stay here, you are welcome to."

Something in her gaze softened, and she reached up to touch his face. "Liron, I'm not saying, 'I want to be yours until I get bored.' I'm not going to do what Elizabeth did."

He flinched at the mere mention of her name and looked down. The thought of Melody abandoning him was a hundred times worse than when his former wife had walked out on him. In such a short amount of time, she had wrapped herself around him that much.

She sighed and continued to touch his face, his chest, his shoulders. Anywhere her hands fell, she soothed and caressed. He closed his eyes, holding those precious touches close to his heart. "I don't know how much you know about the human world, but where I come from, many people spend their lives feeling like they don't really belong anywhere. Like they are alone, an oddity. The only time I ever felt like I truly belonged was when I was surrounded by music. When I went to Juilliard, when I would play in the orchestra, when I would compose. Being lost within the notes and the sweeping sound felt like home to me. And I shared it with my parents, so I never felt lost or alone.

"When they died, it was like I could never get back to that place again. It felt hollow and cold when I tried. Liron, it wasn't until I found you and came here that I felt that again. That safety and sense of belonging. It no longer exists in my world. It exists with you. Maybe by human standards, it doesn't make sense, but I don't even care. I've fallen in love with you, and I'm starting to realize that maybe I just think more like a muse."

Liron's heart tripped over itself at her words. Could she really love him? Because of his disastrous marriage, he had begun to think he was incapable of being loved. Could someone as wonderful, as inspiring and lovely as Melody, really want him? The realization that she wanted to give him everything he had longed for and been denied was overwhelming.

He sighed and leaned in to rest his forehead against hers. "It's the strangest thing," he murmured. "I was paired with Elizabeth as my perfect muse mate. We were supposed to inspire one another and, in turn, inspire humans. She was unhappy with her life, her world, her arrangement with me. She wanted riches and grandeur and a short life full of material things and fame. Then, a human woman walks into my world, full of passion and beauty, with a connection to me that is so strong I hear compositions when she enters the room. Elizabeth abandoned me because she thought like a human and wanted a human life. At random, I was given a human who thinks like a muse. And not just any muse. The perfect one for me."

She snuggled closer to him. "Maybe I was misplaced for a while. Now, I finally found home again."

His breath caught in his throat and emotion overwhelmed him like a tidal wave. He wrapped his arms around her and held her close. She felt perfect against him, and his heart was so full. "Stay with me," he whispered, burying his hands in her golden hair. "Stay with me always. Be mine. My mate, my inspiration, my song."

She pulled back to look up at him and grinned. "Liron Tabor, I thought you'd never get around to actually asking me. I refused to be the one to propose to you."

He laughed and claimed her lips with his again.

"So, when do we get to do it?" she asked.

He pulled back and frowned in bewilderment. "Pardon?"

She grasped his hands in hers. "Let's do it now!"

His lust-induced brain was having difficulty latching onto what she was actually talking about. "Do...what exactly?"

She frowned. "Well, you said all we had to do was find two witnesses and claim each other or something, right?"

Muse marriage...that's what she was referring to. Right. He shook his head to clear his thoughts. "Yes."

"Well, let's go!"

"Now?" She may have thought like a muse, but her time frame still existed on human. "Melody, it's the middle of the night. You haven't slept in almost an entire day and you had a very emotional evening. Do you really think it's best to—?"

"No, *you* haven't slept. I slept for a couple hours when I went back home. But that's because my entire day took up like two hours or whatever in your world. And what are you trying to tell me? That you don't want to do it?"

At the sly way her eyebrow raised, he was beginning to wonder if she was intentionally making his thoughts go south. His body raged like an inferno, and he briefly considered if any of this was a good idea. She could very well kill him by the end of all of this. His blood could reach a degree that was impossible for his body to sustain and he could spontaneously combust. Or, given the fact that he'd been celibate for a really long time by both human and muse standards, he could have a heart attack right there, if he even remembered how to make love to a woman at all. It wasn't like Elizabeth had given him much practice.

"Liron?" She shook his hand and frowned at him, concern that he might actually be changing his mind flashing over her lovely features.

His heart melted and all doubts vanished from his mind as love for her chased them all away. He took her face in his hands and kissed her, then pulled back and grinned. "All right, let's go."

Chapter Fourteen

The woman who came to the door of the house that Liron and Melody invaded looked like she had literally just crawled out of bed. Her brown hair was sticking up in about five different directions, and she was rubbing groggily at her puffy eyes.

"Hi!" Melody greeted. Behind the woman, a man came trudging up, his red stocking cap making him look very gnome-like. "Oh, good! There are two of you!" She squeezed Liron's hand and suppressed a giggle. His rich, quiet chuckle inflamed her, and the joy she felt surge to life within her heart was overpowering.

She turned to face him and shook his hand. "Go on," she urged.

He raised an eyebrow. "Me first?"

"Well, sure. I don't know what I'm doing!"

He grinned and reached out to tuck back an errant strand of her hair. "Melody...uh...." He frowned in question.

"Hoffman," she supplied.

"Melody Hoffman, I claim you as my mate, my inspiration and chosen one." The warmth in his gaze was almost tangible.

His words seemed to flow through her and take root in her heart, and she closed her eyes, letting out a shaky breath. If she didn't know any better, she would have sworn that they actually filled a place within her that had been waiting for them, for him, forever. None of it made any sense.

None of it had to.

She opened her eyes and looked up at him. She lost herself within the bottomless depth of his gaze, and while none of this was how she had ever envisioned herself getting married, nothing had ever felt more natural and right to her. "Liron Tabor," she murmured. "I claim you as my mate...my inspiration and my chosen one." The joy on his face was like the sunrise to her. She stared at him for a long moment, feeling such peace, such contented wonder, when she looked into his eyes.

The man cleared his throat suddenly. "Are you two finished? Because, with all due respect, we'd like to go back to sleep now."

Melody and Liron turned to face the groggy couple. She glanced back up at Liron. "Are we finished?" It was all so simple. Could things in life really be that simple? You feel creative? Then create something. You love someone? Just tell them and you're legally married. You're emotional? It's perfectly acceptable. The philosophy was so hard for her to wrap her mind around, but her heart embraced it as the most natural thing in the universe.

Liron nodded that they were indeed finished, and he took her hand to lead her away from the small, thatched hut they had run to closest to Liron's home. The couple shut the door and Melody turned, followed Liron down the sandy path to the cliffs for several paces, then stopped in bewilderment. She felt like her brain was having a difficult time catching up with reality.

"Oh my gosh," she murmured. "I'm your wife."

He turned to face her, alarm clouding his beautiful face. "Do you regret your decision?"

She shook her head emphatically. "No, no, it's just...." She shook her head again as it seemed to be the only action capable of expressing how rattled her mind felt. She looked up at him and smiled. "People don't do things like that in my world. Ever. I mean, not unless they're drunk and in Vegas." He arched an eyebrow in mild confusion. She giggled and took his hand, twining their fingers as she continued to stroll down to the shore.

"Humans have a constant battle between mind and heart," she explained. "We are taught that what we feel is treacherous. It can get us into trouble if we follow our emotions without thinking them through. And, for the most part, that's true in my world. Blindly following your emotions can get you into a wealth of trouble where I come from. The human world is full of lies and deceit and people taking advantage of others."

"We have that here as well, Melody," he interrupted. "Caution is a necessary part of life in any dimension, but muses are creative beings. And in order to create, we must embrace our emotions. Emotion is vital to creation."

She smiled at the simple explanation. Maybe that was why his world appealed to her so much. "With humans, it's much more complicated," she continued. They reached the shore and she bent down to remove her shoes so she could walk in the sand. "For example, tonight, or maybe it was three days ago by now." She shook her head. "Who knows? Time is all messed up for me right now." He laughed softly and his fingers tightened over hers. "Anyway, when I was at that symphony, the piece I heard upset me. I had an emotional meltdown. Here, you held me, you listened to me, you let me cry and let my emotions run their course."

"Well, of course. What else would I do?"

She smiled wryly. "Look at me like you feared for my sanity because it's not 'healthy' to be having such an emotional reaction a year after my parents passed away."

He blinked in obvious bewilderment and frowned. "That's ridiculous. That kind of loss is not something you can eradicate from your being. And grief is something personal. There is no formula for it."

They stopped close by where they had shared their passionate moment before, and Melody sighed as she turned to look at the sea. The water was inky in the darkness and the air was moist and electric. Off in the distance, lightning lit up the sky and made the waves angry and turbulent. A storm was rolling in, but was still far enough away to be of no imminent danger. "I know that, but humans are taught that, if you haven't moved on, you don't know how. Life doesn't stop, so you're not supposed to stop either. Keep busy and you won't hurt. Bury it until it's so far down you forget about it...until you're fifty and it all comes back to kick your butt and you have a nervous breakdown." She rolled her eyes. "Our society is stupid, the philosophies we live by. Emotions are sometimes seen as the enemy, and if you are an emotional creature, and you don't want everyone telling you that you need therapy, you had better learn to hide everything you're feeling behind a great big giant fake smile."

He snorted his displeasure. "I will never ask you to hide what you feel from me."

She turned to face him and smiled. "I know that. I know I don't need to worry about that here. That's why, even

though my human mind, which has been conditioned to never trust my emotions, was screaming at me back there that I
was doing the most impulsive, stupid thing I could have ever
imagined, my heart knew it was right." She stepped closer to
him and ran her palms up his chest in the way he liked. "My
heart has always known you were right. Ever since I played
your music."

His arms encompassed her and his lips met hers in a
tender yet needy kiss that turned her whole body to mush.
The wind picked up, tossing her hair and tugging at her
dress, causing her to mold herself more intimately to Liron.
Something shifted between them, morphing with the realization that they belonged to one another now. No barriers, no
limits, no rules. She was his, and he was hers. And she
couldn't help but feel as if she had been waiting her whole
life for this very moment. This very scene. It was better than
any written song, any composition, for this was the song
created by the rhythm of their hearts beating in tandem. It
was theirs, their song together. He had been the missing
piece of her concerto all along.

Pulling away with a soft breath, Liron looked down into
her eyes and she saw the same longing in his gaze that she
herself felt. Without any words, he took her hand and led her
down the shore to where the craggy cliffs had created a
bridge of sorts. There was a large hole eaten away out of the
rock, open on both ends, but creating a shelter from any kind
of inhospitable weather.

He turned to face her and searched her eyes once again.
Her breath caught at the smoldering desire she saw burning
within his blue gaze, and her heart melted at the silent question that she could still read within it. She let out a soft sigh
and reached up to push his hair back from his face and trail
her fingers down the line of his jaw.

The tender gesture caused him to shiver and he
squeezed his eyes shut, bringing his forehead to rest against
hers. "Melody," he whispered, his voice holding an ache to it.

"Shhh," she breathed, wrapping her arms around his
neck. "I'm not going anywhere. I'm yours now. Always. I
promise." She lifted her lips to his to seal her vow, meaning
it within the very depths of her soul. She didn't care that her
human mind said it was ludicrous and hasty. Her heart knew

it had finally found home.

He took her face in both of his hands as he kissed her, parting her lips to deepen it. She rose on her toes to press herself fully against his strong frame. Lovely, wonderful notes invaded her mind, and she felt their vibrations in every cell of her body.

He slipped his arm around her waist and, with infinite gentleness, lowered her to the soft sand below. He kissed and nibbled at her lips in an unhurried fashion that belied the hunger she felt within him just below the surface. She reached up to tangle her fingers in his hair and banished any lingering doubt from her mind. Whenever she was with Liron, everything else fell away.

"You are such a gift," he whispered as he kissed his way down her throat and across her collarbone. "I don't know what I did to end up with such a perfect present."

She smiled. "You wrote a music score that spoke to my heart," she murmured. Her fingers absently trailed over the buttons of his shirt and began to undo them.

He sat back and hastily removed the garment, throwing it off to the side and smiling softly down at her. "That score *was* my heart."

She sat up and ran her hands up his chest, delighting in how much more sinful the simple touch was when her fingers were gliding over his bare skin. He was all lithe muscle, lean and elegant.

He shivered. "I don't know what it is about when you do that. It makes all my thoughts scatter."

She grinned and pressed soft kisses here and there, without an agenda, just wanting to feel and taste his skin. She slid her hands around to his back and twined her arms around him, resting her cheek on his chest. She closed her eyes and sighed in contentment. "Your heart is a symphony, Liron."

His arms tightened around her for a moment before he took her face in his hands and tilted her lips up to meet his. He claimed them in a fierce, impassioned kiss, his tongue marauding her mouth in a primal, wild dance that made her heartbeat trip over itself in its attempt to accelerate so quickly.

He guided her back down onto the sand and she tangled her fingers in his hair as he explored her mouth. After a few moments, he pulled away just enough to cause her to protest. He smiled down at her and caressed her cheek before lowering his lips so that they hovered just above hers. She could feel his breath, and with every warm exhale that touched her lips, the softest, faintest sounds of whispering music filtered through her. She closed her eyes and fidgeted, trying to seal the kiss he was teasing her with. She wanted to feel the velvet softness of his lips, wanted to satiate her hunger for him, as well as for the music she couldn't quite hear completely.

His low chuckle caused a louder burst of notes in her mind, and they traveled through her like electricity, lighting her ablaze for the rest of the song and the rest of its creator.

Instead of kissing her lips as she had anticipated, Liron turned his attention to her collarbone. He pressed a gentle kiss there, and she sucked her breath in as another measure of music cavorted through her body, heart, and mind.

With deliberate slowness, he ran his palm across her bare shoulder and down the feminine curves of her body. She almost convulsed at the river of fire and erotic music he left in his wake.

His hand stopped at her knee, where he hooked his fingers behind it and bent her leg. The skirt of her dress slithered down her skin to gather at her waist, and his musical caress followed the path of the fabric. Her breath caught as her body began to feel like an orchestra of its own. Everywhere he touched, a different part of her being came alive with a different sound. Her mind filled with the most amazing melodies of his heart while her body burned in a slow ache.

She barely felt him pull her dress over her head. The cold ocean air hitting her bare skin was the only indication, but he quickly took the chill away with the infernal caress of his hands and lips. She squirmed, trying to find some sort of coherent thought within the maelstrom of notes and sensations he built with every erotic sweep of his fingers, lips, and tongue. Her fingers tangled in his hair while his mouth explored her body in an unhurried journey that was going to drive her insane.

"Liron," she managed to rasp out, tugging gently on the silky strands. "I can't think...this isn't fair."

His low chuckle was like the rumble of a kettledrum. He dragged his lips in a slow line of kisses up her throat. "What isn't fair?"

"I...." She struggled to remember how to verbalize while his hands did wicked things. "I want to touch you too, but I can't even..." She groaned as another wave of sultry music pulsed through her.

"Shhh," he breathed against her ear. "There will be time for that later."

"But..." She gasped as he blanketed her body with his, and somewhere in the back of her mind, she realized he had managed to discard the rest of both of their clothing. When that had happened, she had no idea. His hips nestled against hers, and she shivered.

"We have many nights and days ahead of us that we can explore one another, if you so desire," he whispered. "For now, please give me this chance to show you what you mean to me."

He kissed her long and thorough, and every nerve in her body thrummed with a song of its own—his song. She opened her eyes and forced herself to focus through the haze of passion and feeling that swept through her. The way he had said that statement, *"if you so desire,"* made her heart ache. He was still afraid that she would not want him after this, that there was something about him that had turned Elizabeth off and that he would do the same to her. How could he think that? More importantly, how could Elizabeth have spurned him when he had the power to make someone feel so much? He had loved her, which meant he had lavished this same kind of affection on her. How could she have felt nothing? Melody thought she was going to explode inside a cyclone of sensations. How could Elizabeth have just endured that instead of falling so hard for him at the realization that he'd felt so much for her?

Melody both hated and loved Liron's ex-wife. She hated her for hurting Liron, but she rejoiced in the fact that because of her idiocy, he now belonged to Melody. And she knew it might take some time to convince him completely, but she would make him realize how incredible he was, in every way. He would come to never doubt her feelings for him, or how talented and desirable he really was. No one else had ever made her feel the way he did, not in the smallest measurement. She was lost, and she was addicted. Addicted to his touch, his heart, and his resplendent song.

She gazed into his blue eyes. They had turned stormy with his passion, mirroring the turbulent sea. Lightning lit up the sky as the storm moved closer, and thunder rumbled low and ominous. Behind them, the waves crashed. It seemed the whole world was making music, taking part in the overture that Liron was creating just for her.

He reached behind him to grasp one of her legs and bend it at the knee, sliding his fingers across her skin in a decadent, velvet caress that made what little rational thought she had fly away into the night. He settled himself more intimately against her and dropped a slow, languorous kiss to her lips.

When he pulled back, he took her hand and placed her palm over his heart. She surfaced enough from the haze of feeling she was trapped within to look up into his beautiful face. All she saw there was devotion and desire, complete and total rapture. For her. It was so overwhelming she felt tears burn behind her eyes.

But before the emotion could take over, he lowered his lips to hers again and claimed her body with his, sending such a tremendous wave of wonderful sound sweeping through her that she didn't even recognize the noise that was torn from her throat. She shuddered and clutched him close to her while he buried his face against her neck and let out a shaky breath. He whispered her name like it was the most cherished word he had ever spoken, and she felt her heart beating in tandem with his, playing the same wonderful song. The music that made up his person surged into her, connecting them on every available level.

Lightning flickered again overhead, followed by the gentle roll of thunder. The rhythm of the ocean waves seemed to match the rhythm of Liron's body against hers and the tempo of their synchronized heartbeats. The music she felt and heard, along with the tremendous pleasure rippling through her with every movement Liron made, coalesced into one symphonic masterpiece. It coiled tighter within her, took over all of her senses, and she lost herself within the sound and the passion as all of the elements climbed toward crescendo.

She'd never felt anything like it as the realm of reality fractured and dissolved into a world full of nothing but the purest music and burning emotion. At that moment, *she* was the music and he, the conductor. She was lost to him in every way. Her heart, her body, the song of her soul—all of it belonged to him.

After what felt like an eternity of slow boiling, burning, erotic musical sensation, every note within Melody converged with the physical pleasure of Liron's lovemaking and exploded inside her like white-hot energy. She arched her back and dug her fingers into his shoulders as wave after wave of ecstatic light and sound crashed over her.

She expected the feeling to ebb, but it didn't. Liron kissed her, never breaking the pulsing sonata that coursed through her blood and wrapped around her heart and every part of her body. Melody whimpered and writhed against him, certain that she would incinerate if he made her feel any more, but Liron was relentless. He took her over the edge again, bringing to life notes and chords inside of her that she never even knew existed. He turned her entire being into an orchestra, opened up secret chambers in her heart that filled with love for him, and only then did he allow his song to come to completion.

As Melody slowly drifted back into the real world, Liron pulled her up close to him, dropping lazy kisses along her shoulder and neck. Melody couldn't think, could barely function. She snuggled up against Liron and basked in the warm, thrumming sensation that still pulsed throughout her body.

"That...that was...." She couldn't complete the sentence because moving her lips and tongue required too much effort.

His soft chuckle filled her with warmth as he wrapped her up in his arms and nuzzled the back of her neck. "Yes, it was."

She smiled and relaxed against him, enjoying the feel of his skin touching hers, of his arm wrapped around her waist, of knowing she was his. The sky was lightening with the coming of dawn, but dark storm clouds roiled overhead and a drizzling rain began to mist the air.

Melody sighed. They were protected from the weather in their nature-made shelter, and she was in no great hurry to move. For the first time in what seemed like so long, her heart was full and content. She planned on holding onto that for as long as possible.

Chapter Fifteen

She was aware of the rain peppering the stained glass window in Liron's bedroom as she was roused from slumber. She didn't know how long she had slept, only that the warmth of Liron's embrace provided the perfect haven for her to rest.

They had dressed and returned to Liron's home, where they'd bathed and eaten, then climbed into his bed, contented and exhausted. It felt close to evening, and she smiled at the thought that they had slept the day away.

She remained where she was for several minutes, basking in the serenity of the sound of the rain and the feel of Liron's arm wrapped securely around her. She realized this was her bed now, her home. It should have frightened her, with the idea being so foreign, but it didn't. Her heart was happy here, sated, and she had no desire to return to her cold world. There, she was sad, lonely, and condemned for her emotions. Here, she was with Liron, her mate, who understood her and embraced both her emotions and her passion for music. She fit here, and her place in her world had vanished with the death of her parents. There was nothing left for her there now.

Although, she did need to finalize her business, take care of her house and such, and she wanted some of her things. She would have to attend to that the next time the portal opened. But right now, none of that really seemed all that important.

She smiled and turned in Liron's arms. She was dressed only in one of his black button-down shirts, and he was in black boxer shorts, another strange and modern thing in Liron's half-medieval world. The random occurrence of indoor plumbing, modern clothing and furniture, certain technology, and other things that seemed out of place in a world with taverns, outdoor marketplaces, and horses instead of cars surprised her, but she imagined it would take her awhile to discover everything about Liron's world. It was an adventure she looked forward to.

Liron's hair was fanned out across his pillow in a dark, beautiful disarray and Melody reached up to brush back an errant lock that had fallen across his forehead. She snuggled closer to him and pressed a kiss to the hollow of his throat.

He stirred and the arm he had around her waist tightened. A soft smile lifted his lips even though he didn't open his eyes. "Oh good," he murmured. "It wasn't just a fantasy I created after all."

She grinned and ran her hand over his bare shoulder and across his chest. "Not unless I had the same fantasy."

He shrugged lazily, still not opening his eyes. "I am a muse, you know. I'm supposed to create things. Maybe I created you so I didn't have to sleep alone anymore."

"Hmm," she teased, pushing him onto his back and rolling over so she was straddling his hips. His eyes flew open, and he sucked in his breath. She giggled. "Well, if I was a figment of your imagination, would you be able to feel this?" She wiggled her hips, settling herself against him provocatively.

He groaned and reached up to bury his fingers in her hair. "You had better be careful doing that. This shirt I loaned you might not be on you very much longer."

She gave him her best seductive look and began to slowly loosen the buttons. "I'm not seeing any kind of negative in that option."

Surprise flashed across his features, and her heart melted. She wondered how long it would take to convince him that she was really here for the long haul, and that she found him to be the most desirable man she had ever met.

She undid the last button and leaned forward so her lips teased over his. "Yes, Liron," she murmured. "I still want you."

Burning desire and smoldering devotion filled his eyes, and he took her in his arms, rolling her onto her back. "You're playing with fire, Mrs. Tabor," he said, his voice husky.

Warm giddiness filled her at the mention of her new name. She wondered if she would have to change it in his world. She guessed not, since there were no records of her ever being there. She even imagined she wouldn't need to mess with the legalities in her own world. It wasn't like she was going to be there long enough for it to matter.

"I like fire," she teased. "Especially the kind you create." She reached up to thread her fingers through his hair. She frowned in thought. "Not to bring up an uncomfortable subject, but how in the world did Elizabeth not become putty in your hands after you made love to her?"

Liron's striking face tinged pink with a blush, and she giggled. He cocked an eyebrow at her and slipped his hand inside her open shirt to push the fabric off of her shoulder. He kissed her there lazily. "Elizabeth was cold as ice. I imagine she can't be faulted completely. If she didn't have feelings for me, that was all there was to it."

"Still... Do muses feel things the same way humans do? I mean, I know I can't make you hear music like you do, but—"

He cut her off by placing his fingers to her lips. "You make me hear scores," he murmured. "You make me hear wonder untold. You inspire me in a way only muses are supposed to be able to. You are a miracle. Stop worrying."

She closed her eyes as his lips trailed down her neck and over her exposed shoulder. "I'm not worried. I'm just...saying." She sighed and any point she had been trying to make died as his mouth continued its descent.

"You want to know what you make me hear?" he whispered. "I'll show you." One of his hands traveled down her side to her hip, and the notes that filled her mind were wicked and wonderful. She groaned and sought his lips with hers, surrendering to his music and his masterful touch.

It was a lovely, warm day as Melody and Liron wandered through the marketplace. Liron couldn't remember the last time his heart had felt so content and full. He had grown accustomed to the aching hollowness of his solitude. Having Melody with him, holding his hand as they shopped for her new wardrobe, was so simple, but spoke so much. Where Elizabeth had spurned and shunned him, regardless of what he had done for her, Melody accepted him, embraced him, *wanted* him. She made all of his dreams and wildest fantasies come true in blazing color and sound.

"I'm hungry," she announced suddenly, turning to look up at him. "Can we stop to get some lunch?"

He smiled and gave a nod. "Of course. Let's go this way. I know of a nice place."

"Hopefully somewhere that I won't get hog slop spilled down my front."

He looked back at her and smothered a chuckle at the odd outfit she had dressed in. Considering she couldn't fit in any of his pants, she had put her dress on from the night before, but buttoned his black shirt up over it. Thus, the purpose of the shopping excursion.

As they headed down a small alley, Liron stopped short as he came face to face with Melody's living room splayed out in front of him with a rather insistent pounding at her door. He frowned. "It seems someone desires your attention...again." He didn't mean to sound so dismal when he said it, but something strange made his heart squeeze in his chest.

Melody moved around him to see for herself. "It's probably Nikki. I knew, sooner or later, she would come to check up on me again. And who knows how long it's been in my world." She turned to face him and put her hands on his chest. "This actually comes at a great time. I can go home, get some clothing, and tie up all my loose ends."

His brow furrowed as the uneasy feeling inside of him intensified. "I'll come with you."

She shook her head. "It's okay, Liron. I won't be long. Really not long by your time standards. Only long enough to get my stuff squared away, and I want some pictures of my family and things."

He took her hands in his and rubbed his thumbs over the backs of them. How could he tell her that he didn't feel right? That, this time, something felt off? Was he just being paranoid? Afraid to lose her now that he had her?

The pounding on her door intensified, and he met her gaze. "You're sure you don't want me to come with you?" He couldn't put a reason to his uneasiness, not one that would hold merit.

"I don't even know if you could cross into my world through that portal. Maybe I'm the only one who can. It'll be fine. I'll be back in no time." She rose up to kiss his lips softly. "And when I come back, I'll be all yours."

His heart fluttered at the thought of having her forever, but it did little to chase away the foreboding that was gripping him. "Please don't be gone long," he whispered.

She shook her head. "I promise, just long enough to get my business in order." She kissed him again. "I love you."

Her words pierced him like an arrow, and he choked on his reply as she turned and headed through the portal. She had barely stepped through it before it swallowed her, leaving only the dismal, empty alleyway behind.

Melody was grinning as she ran to her door. She couldn't wait to tell Nikki more about Liron. Although, she would have to leave out the random eloping part. She didn't think her friend would necessarily understand that. And she really didn't want to bring up the part about her deciding to go live in another dimension. But hey, she could tell her some of the other good stuff. Nikki didn't need to know all the technicalities.

She yanked the door open only to have her smile fizzle like a burnt out sparkler. It wasn't Nikki. It was friggin' Rob. Of all the people she *didn't* want to see. Her good mood vanished, and she crossed her arms with a scowl. "What do you want, Rob?"

The glower on his face was ferocious, and he pushed his way into her door without even waiting for an invite. "What do I want? Nice way to greet your boyfriend after disappearing into thin air for a week. Where the hell have you been, Melody?"

She blinked rapidly because her brain had difficulty catching up with all of that. *Boyfriend? In his twisted dreams.* And he was swearing at her now. Nice. She heaved a sigh and let her front door slam shut. "Last time I checked, you weren't my boyfriend. Like, ever. Actually, the last time I saw you, you were just an ass telling me I was being overly dramatic about my parents dying."

He snorted. "Whatever. I'm not going to listen to you whine about that right now. I want some answers. I'm not going to ask you again. I'm sick of this cat-and-mouse, hard-to-get dance of yours. Where have you been?"

She stared at him. Gaped was actually a better word. Okay, enough was enough. She was sick of this man. *Really* sick of him. She let out a long-suffering sigh. "All right, Rob. You want an explanation? Fine. Since you're obviously denser than a brick, let me spell it out for you. I'm not interested in you. I do not want to be with you. Not now, not tomorrow, not ever. You have the compassion of a cockroach and are just about as appealing to me as one. Besides that, I've met someone."

"You *what*?" His face turned an angry shade of red and a vein bulged in his neck.

"Yes, in case you didn't know, there are other people in the world that I prefer to you and your overstuffed ego."

"Who is it?"

"I told you already. It's the composer of that music Nikki bought me. That just happens to be a really weathered piece of music." It was basically true. "Not that it's any of your business."

The vein continued to bulge while a muscle ticked in his jaw. "You know, this music obsession of yours is absolutely out of control. You need to get a grip."

"*I* need to get a grip?" She choked out a laugh. "You know what you need to do? You need to get out of my house!" She stabbed her finger toward the door.

"I can't believe you'd entertain some fantasy about some stupid musician when you have me right in front of you." He shook his head with another snort. "Screw this. I'm taking care of this once and for all. This music crap has gone too far." He strode over to the piano before she realized what he was doing.

Her eyes widened as he snatched Liron's score and headed into the kitchen. She ran after him, but his swiftness was insane. By the time she caught up to him, he'd already pulled out a cigarette lighter and lit the corner of the score like a torch. Because of the age of the brittle paper, it went up like dry grass. She screamed and watched in horror as her connection to Liron and his world burnt to cinders and ash while Rob dropped it in her sink.

She stared for several heartbeats, which sounded like thunder in her ears.

"Now maybe you'll stop being a baby, get over all this

stupidity about music and your parents, and realize what you have in front of you," Rob spat. "I'm sick of being put on the backburner for your little games."

Terrific, blinding rage swept through her with the force of a volcano. With a half-scream, half-growl she barely recognized as coming out of her own throat, she strode to Rob, pulled her arm back and socked him a good one. Her fist made contact with the hard line of his jaw and actually snapped his head back. The utter shock on his face should have appeased her somewhat, but all she wanted to do was hit him again, then again and again until he was black and blue. And after that, she wanted to yank every last piece of his hair out.

"*Get out!*" she bellowed.

The shocked expression didn't leave his face, but he didn't move either.

With another primal snarl, she snatched a butcher knife out of her knife block and wielded it at him threateningly. "You have exactly two seconds to get the *hell* out of my house before I cut your balls off right here in my kitchen!" She advanced a step and must have looked as crazed as she felt because he dashed out of her path and around to the doorway of the kitchen.

"Melody, what are you doing? Are you insane?"

"I told you to get out!" She started toward him, still clutching the knife. "If you think I'm joking, go ahead and try me!"

He made a hasty retreat out the front door, still muttering protests. She followed after him until she could lock her screen and assure herself he couldn't get back in.

"If I *ever* see you on my property again, I'm getting a restraining order. Do not come over here. Do not call me. Do not stand across the street and holler. If you do"—she waved the knife again—"I'll say it was self-defense." She slammed the inner door so hard it shook the frame.

The silence of her empty house was deafening, and she dropped the knife to the ground as she started to tremble. Her rage abated into panic and a strangled sob escaped her throat as she ran to her piano.

She sat down and tried to remember Liron's score. She closed her eyes, forced the overwhelming panic down, and focused on the notes. She had played the score by feeling alone in the past. She could do so now.

She blundered through the first few measures, but then it all disappeared. She tried again, and again, but she couldn't remember, and the more she tried, the more of it slipped away. It was like the connection had just vanished, and along with it, her ability to play the song based solely on the emotions the music created.

Finally, she slammed her fingers down on the keys with a thunderous crash and screamed as her panic turned into the all-consuming sorrow of utter loss. She had no way to reach Liron now. She wouldn't be able to access the portal without the music. She couldn't get home! He was her home now. His world was her home. And she couldn't get back!

Her heart splintered and shattered like it had when she'd found out her parents had died, and she let out an otherworldly cry that didn't sound human. She wrapped her arms around herself, as if doing so could hold all the pieces of her heart in place. She rocked back and forth on the piano bench, sobbing uncontrollably.

The one piece of happiness she had found after feeling nothing but emptiness had been ripped from her. And the gaping chasm it left within her was so much worse than she remembered.

Where Liron had filled her with light and beauty, dark coldness seeped in like a disease. The man she loved and the future she had finally been able to see for herself were hopelessly out of her grasp now, and she had no idea how to get them back.

Her house suddenly felt like a prison, and she felt utterly, bitterly alone.

Chapter Sixteen

Liron paced in agitation across his living room floor. Something was wrong. He felt it in every part of him. Muses had a telepathic connection to the humans they inspired, and he could feel Melody's emotions—horrible loss and devastating pain, sorrow and rage. He ran his fingers through his hair and growled out a frustrated sound. She had been gone for half the day, which meant it had to have at least been twenty-four hours in her world, if not more.

He had been barraged by her intense distress almost as soon as she'd gone through the portal. It hadn't abated and he'd been slowly going insane knowing that she was hurting, but he was unable to do anything about it. He knew he should have listened to his instincts, should have gone through the portal with her. What if she was hurt? What could have happened to make his Melody so distraught?

He finally abandoned the pacing and sat down in a chair, and for another agonizing hour, he endured her pain before it quietly dwindled in its intensity. That fact alone snapped him to action. The fact that her emotions had abated meant that she had to have finally gone to sleep, which meant he could connect with her.

He bolted out into the sunset and hurried to the beach where he and Melody had made love. All creatures had an energy signature, and it was that which he needed to connect with in order to find her through the telepathic link they shared. It would be easier and faster for him to lock onto her energy signature in a place where they had been connected and in tune with one another.

It was brisk with the evening fog, and he made a hasty fire out of driftwood in order to stave off the chill. He had to concentrate in order to find Melody and speak with her in her dreams, and he couldn't afford the distraction of being cold.

Once his fire was going strong, Liron sat down across from it, closed his eyes, and tapped into his talent, one he hadn't used in such a very long time. He went deep into his mind, letting his senses heighten and fan out, transcending the barrier between his realm and the human world, to detect Melody's unique song amidst the sea of sound. Because he was a music muse, Liron heard humans' energy signatures as songs. Each person had a different song, and he had to sift through them to find the one that was Melody's and Melody's alone.

He didn't know how long he searched for her. It could have been minutes. It could have been hours. But, finally, he detected the soft, wonderful notes that signaled his wife. They were faint, tinkling, and light. She sounded like wind chimes and sunshine, like happiness and life.

He locked onto the sound and pushed his mind toward her energy signature, invading it and wrapping his own around it, hoping he could reach her and get her to listen to him. He would only be able to speak with Melody if she let him, if she recognized him. He hoped with all his heart that she would. He couldn't bear feeling her pain any longer and being helpless to do anything about it.

Melody could hear the sea. The waves were crashing against the shore with a rhythmic beauty that called to her. It sounded like Liron, all power and elegance, nature's music in its purest form. She tried to nestle into the sound, wrap it around herself, and lose herself in the wonderful memory it brought to mind.

Suddenly, she was there, sitting on the beach where she and Liron had made love. It was sunset, and the sky was tinted with pink and purple. She blinked in bewilderment and trailed her fingers through the sand, but felt nothing. It was as if she was in some strange and tormenting mirage. Horrible loss and pain weighed on her heart and she pulled her knees to her chest.

"Melody."

She jerked her head up and looked around, confused, her heart beating hard.

"Melody, can you hear me?"

She stood and spun around, looking for him, knowing his voice, but she could see nothing but the waves and the shore. "Liron?" she murmured.

She swore she heard him heave a sigh. *"Thank goodness."* His voice had an echoing, otherworldly quality to it, as if he was everywhere and nowhere.

She frowned and stepped forward. "Where are you? Where am I? Why can't I feel the sand beneath my feet? Nothing has any solidity to it. What's going on?" She felt frantic, afraid she was somehow caught between her world and his. What would happen if she got stuck there? Would she float around in this half-existence forever?

"Melody, listen to me. You're dreaming."

She blinked. "I am?"

"Yes. I found you through the telepathic connection we share. A muse can contact humans this way, through dreams. We use this method to impart visions, or words, music, whatever we need in order to inspire. I have never had to do this with you, as you have always come to me physically."

Horrendous despair clutched at her heart while, at the same time, she basked in the knowledge that she could communicate with him. Tears filled her eyes and spilled down her cheeks. "Liron, I can't get home."

"What has happened? I can feel your distress and it's killing me."

"It was Rob. He freaked out on me, was pissed because I dumped him, even though we were never really together in the first place. H-He burned your score, Liron! That was the key to accessing the portal! I don't know how to get back! I tried to play your music from memory, but I couldn't." She wiped at her eyes, aching to be in his arms. He was so close, but just out of her reach.

"Shhh. Please stop crying, lovely. It's breaking my heart. Everything will be fine. I promise. Are you hurt? Did he harm you?"

His voice went from soft to holding a harsh bite in 2.5 seconds. His protectiveness brought a small smile to her lips. She shook her head. "No, he didn't hurt me. Actually, I almost hurt him. I chased him out of my house with a butcher knife." His rich laughter surprised her, but rumbled around her like thunder and soothed some of the ache in her heart. Her bottom lip trembled nonetheless. "I tried all day and most of the night to get back to you," she murmured. "It was terrible. Every time I tried to play your song, I forgot more and more of it. I was afraid I was never going to see you again. I don't know what time it was when I finally fell asleep. I was so exhausted."

"I wish you had fallen asleep sooner. I couldn't come to you until you did. Humans think too much when they are awake. Their logic overrides everything. The subconscious is what opens the mind enough to let muses in. Why do you think so many artists, writers, and musicians keep notepads by their beds? To write down their dreams. Dreams are what inspire them because we speak to them in dreams. We show them what they need in order to create."

She shook her head. "I'm sorry. I didn't know."

"Of course you didn't, lovely. I'm not reprimanding you. I'm just informing you."

"How did you know I had fallen asleep?"

"I could feel your strong emotions. It was terrible to endure them when I didn't know what was happening. All I knew was that you were in pain and I couldn't get to you. When they subsided, I knew your mind was finally resting."

Tears burned again. "I thought I'd lost you. I thought I'd never be able to find you again."

"There will be none of that. You cannot marry me and then discard me so easily."

She smiled in spite of herself and wished she could touch him and see his blue eyes.

"Things have become a little more complicated is all. Do you think my music score would open the portal if you could remember it?"

"I think so. That was always how I was able to come back to your world before."

"All right then. I am going to put the music in your mind. It should be there when you awaken, like an annoying song you can't get out of your head."

Her smile grew ever so slightly. "Your music could never be an annoying song, Liron. Your music is magnificent. It's not like you're some pop star or something." His chuckle warmed her.

"Play the music when you wake up. If the portal opens and you are able to return to me, wait for me once you get here. I am going to talk to someone about a plan B."

She frowned. "Plan B?"

"Yes. I know for a fact there is a way for muses to travel to the human world. I know someone who can help me with that. If you can't get back to me, I will come to you. I promise."

His words filled her with relief and joy. To know that they weren't irrevocably separated was a burden lifted from her battered heart. "Thank you, Liron. I was so afraid."

"You can't get rid of me that easy. Now, sleep. I will send my music to you. And I will hope to see you soon."

She sighed. "When I get back to you, I'm never leaving your side again."

"That is a promise I fully intend to make you keep."

She didn't want him to go. She trusted him, but didn't want to feel like he had vanished into oblivion. What if none of this worked? What if they couldn't get back to one another? She had ruined everything. He had wanted to come back with her. Why hadn't she let him? She thought she could play with the laws of physics forever and they would just bend to her will? How stupid was she?

"Lovely, why are you so upset? I can feel your turmoil again. Please, believe me. If you cannot come to me, I will find a way to you. I admit I am a selfish man. I refuse to live without the rapturous music you fill me with."

Her anxiety quieted and she smiled, forcing a calming breath into her lungs. "That's a promise I intend to make *you* keep."

His laughter was faint; it sounded like he was fading. *"Rest now. All will be well. I love you."*

A rogue tear streaked down her cheek against her will. "I love you too, Liron."

She awoke with a startled gasp and sat up in bed. She frowned and searched her mind for Liron's music, but couldn't locate it. With an annoyed growl, she lay back down and flipped over on her side. Yeah, so her traitorous body woke up before he could give her his music. Awesome.

She closed her eyes and tried to fight against the grief and pain of being separated from him, of the nagging possibility in the back of her mind that none of this was going to work, that it had all been a fantasy and she was alone again.

The fact that she still wore his shirt was an anchor. It was real, therefore he was real. She clutched it closer to her, breathing deep the cedar and violin rosin smell that was uniquely Liron. It calmed her, and she imagined she could feel him sleeping beside her. He would be with her soon. It wasn't a fantasy, not a delusion. He would put his music in her mind and she would open the portal again. They would be together soon. He wasn't going to vanish like her parents had. This was not the same.

She repeated those things over and over to make herself believe them and to stave off her irrational fear of abandonment and loneliness. She would not go back to that dark chasm of hopelessness she had been in before finding Liron. All would be well.

All she had to do was trust Liron. Trust he knew what he was talking about and trust the love they had for one another. Their connection had been powerful enough to transcend the boundary between their worlds once. It would happen again. And when it did, she could return to his world and begin her new life there. A life full of creativity and music and fresh adventures. A life with her muse by her side.

Slowly, as she focused on the possibilities for her future, she drifted off into sleep. As she slipped back into the place where only dreams reside, the first few haunting notes of Liron's beautiful score filtered through her mind.

Liron tried to ignore the slightly nauseous feeling in his stomach as he approached the inner courtyard of an estate he had not set eyes on in so long it felt like it had been another lifetime. He paused to stare up at the three-story mansion, sprawling and pretentious, a blatant flaunting of wealth. He sighed and briefly debated turning around and heading back the direction he'd come, but he knew he couldn't. Not when Melody was trapped in the human world, depending on him should his music fail to open the portal.

He drew in a deep breath and forged ahead, walking the cobbled path up to the front door, where he knocked loudly.

He only waited for a few moments before the door opened to reveal a lovely woman with dark hair and sapphire eyes.

Those eyes widened upon seeing him, shock mirrored in their depths.

Liron gave her a small smile. "Hello, Samantha."

The surprise didn't fade from her delicate features. "Liron," she murmured. "Hello. How are you? It's been...so long."

He dipped his head in a slight nod. "It has..." There was a moment of awkward silence before he sucked in a breath and continued. "The reason I'm here—"

At the same exact moment, Samantha spoke. "What can I do for you?"

They both stopped at the same time and Liron smiled softly, some of his apprehension dissipating. This was not days gone by. This was a different time, a different place, a different life. All that had once been had long since vanished. "Samantha, I need your help with something."

A small, worried frown creased her alabaster brow and she stepped aside. "With what? Please, come in."

"Thank you." Liron entered the parlor and looked around. Nothing was the same as he remembered, but why should it be? The estate had gone to Samantha and her husband long ago. It was her home now, not her parents'. Sometimes, memories remained so pristine and untouched in the vaults of one's mind that regardless of the logical fact that life went on, it seemed strange that those memories should be altered over time.

He took a brief glance around at all the polished wood furniture and gleaming marble floors, then faced Samantha, who still looked at him rather strangely. She was dressed in a flowing, elegant blue gown with diamonds glistening at her throat and her earlobes, not to mention the small planet she had on her ring finger. It seemed surreal that he had once been part of this grandeur, this...fluff.

His family had never been impoverished by any means, but they had never been this well off either. It had all seemed so remarkable back then, like an amazing dream. Now, it all just seemed like gold plating on something that was empty inside. Once, maybe, he had desired the finery and the riches, the social gatherings, the parties. It had all seemed like a grand adventure.

Status was not of great importance amongst muses, not when so much time was spent indulging in creativity. But for the ones who were extremely successful in their craft, extravagance was not unusual.

Liron had been intrigued by that lifestyle, for it had differed from his own. Born to a logic muse and a science muse, his parents had spent their time dissecting things, inventing things, and debating with one another. He'd felt relatively out of place for most of his life. But to be introduced to a family full of nothing but music muses, theatre muses, art muses, and writing muses...well, it had all seemed like some kind of fairy tale at the time. He had been hopelessly enamored.

Now, give him a stroll on the beach at sunset and a night spent by the fire with his Melody in his arms. That was all he desired, and all he needed to keep him happy.

He took a deep breath, stopped his meandering thoughts, and faced Samantha again. "Samantha, I need to know how Elizabeth managed to traverse the continuum and get to the human world."

Samantha paled and her expression became slightly pained. "Liron...it's been a very long time. Elizabeth is gone now, both in this world and that one. Don't you think it's time to let the past go?"

"I'm not trying to hang onto the past," he snapped. "I just want to find my wife."

If it was possible, Samantha's concerned expression became even more so, and she approached him to put a consoling hand on his arm. "Liron, she isn't your wife anymore. She hasn't been for...many, many years."

Liron rolled his eyes and shook her hand off his arm as he paced a few agitated lines. "I'm not talking about Elizabeth! I'm talking about Melody! My wife!"

Poor Samantha recoiled as if someone had slapped her. Liron instantly felt remorse for being so scathing to such a gentle woman, and for barking at her things that she would have no way of knowing. He stopped pacing, drew in a calming breath, and faced her.

"O-Oh," she said softly. "I didn't know you had remarried, Liron. Forgive me."

He bestowed her with a small smile. "Of course you wouldn't know that, Samantha. I apologize for snapping at you. I just..." He felt very weary all of a sudden. "I need your help. Melody is human. She somehow managed to end up here, but now she's stuck back in the human world and can't get home. I need to know how to get to her. I know muses have, on occasion, been able to travel to the human world, but Elizabeth is the only one I have ever known personally who actually did it. Please, you're her sister. She told you everything. I know she would have told you about what she was planning. I need to know how she did it so I can find my wife." He met her eyes and knew he looked pleading.

Samantha studied him for a few heartbeats before her eyes softened and she sighed. "Come sit down, Liron. Let me get you something to drink. We'll have a conversation."

He started to follow her down the main corridor when she stopped suddenly and turned back to face him. He raised an eyebrow in mild surprise.

She chewed on her bottom lip and seemed to debate internally for a moment before she met his gaze. "Look, Liron, this probably doesn't mean much, but I need to say it anyway. I never agreed with what Elizabeth did. She was my sister, and I loved her, but what she did to you was deplorable and unacceptable. And not only did she hurt you, she hurt everyone in her family by running off to live a life that had her gone in the blink of an eye. You were always such a kind, gentle man. You didn't deserve the way she treated you."

Liron's heart somersaulted in his chest, and he looked down. He swallowed hard in an attempt to get rid of the lump of emotion that rose in his throat at her validation. He nodded solemnly, then forced himself to meet her eyes again. "Thank you," he rasped. "But none of that matters now. Please, just help me find Melody."

Chapter Seventeen

Melody stared at the closed door, had been staring at it for the past twenty minutes. She knew she had to open it, but apprehension at what would swamp her once she did held her back.

It hadn't been opened since her parents had died. Not since she'd put all of their music equipment, as well as her own—minus the piano—in there the day after the funeral and turned the key in the lock. It was bad enough that she had to walk by it every day, knowing that everything was in there. Everything that had belonged to her parents, everything that had made them happy, everything that had, at one time, given Melody's life color. She knew it was all in there, but she couldn't bear to go in. Not only was it full of memories, but the ghosts were locked in there too. And she knew the ghosts were what would turn her into an emotional wreck.

She took a deep breath and expelled it forcefully, knowing she didn't have a choice. Not after what had been revealed to her over the last twenty-four hours.

She recalled the conversation she'd had with Liron last night.

He had found her in her dreams, once again, on the beach like the last time. She'd been dismal, for though he had given her his music score in her mind, it had failed to open the portal. It had actually failed to do anything except torment her for the entirety of the day, for she played it over and over again until her fingers were sore.

She could hear Liron sigh. *"It must have been the actual score that was the key to the portal,"* he said. *"It was something physical that originated from this world and was still somehow attached to it."*

"But that doesn't make sense!" she cried in frustration. "I was able to go back to my world every time something reminded me of it, or something interrupted me. Why can't it go both ways?"

"Because that is your world, Melody. You originate from there. There is nothing here to pull you back. If I was with you, perhaps it would be different."

"Nothing to pull me back? Liron, *you* should be able to pull me back!" She was aggravated and exhausted, and just wanted to go back home. The longer she was forced to remain in her world, the more depressed she became, and the more she realized how stifled she was here.

"Melody, you were never supposed to actually be in my world. It was a strange phenomenon that you were. Now that the key to opening the portal is destroyed, we are stuck communicating with one another in traditional muse/human fashion. There is only one way to rectify this."

He was silent for so long that Melody's stomach did a back flip. "What is it?" she finally murmured.

"The only way for a muse to enter into the human world is if the human he or she connected to brings them over."

She frowned and waved her hands in impatience. "Okay, fine. So how do I do that?"

"The connection between muse and human has to be incredibly strong."

Why was he stalling? She wished he'd spit it out already. "All right..."

"A muse can only cross over to the human world if his or her human creates something extremely powerful that was inspired by the muse."

She blinked in confusion. "I don't understand exactly. You mean, I have to create something in order to open the portal back up?"

"Yes. The creative connection is what opens the portal. I don't know why and I don't know how. I'm no physicist either. My mother is a scientist. I am not. It has something to do with the energy, I imagine. When and if this works, I will contact her and we can speak with her. I am anxious for you to meet my parents anyway."

Melody smiled, feeling warm all over at the thought of meeting Liron's family and learning more about his life.

"At any rate, my source is very reliable and I trust her."

"Her?" She couldn't keep the note of jealousy out of her voice if she tried.

Liron chuckled. *"Yes, I went to the only person who could possibly know anything about this...Elizabeth's sister."*

Melody raised her eyebrows in surprise. Liron had tracked down his ex-wife's sister in what had to have been an awkward situation to find a way for them to be reunited? Her heart tripped over itself at the thought that she meant that much to him. "So...what exactly am I supposed to create?" She wasn't quite sure she was grasping this concept completely.

He was quiet for a long moment before finally saying, *"I can't help you with that, Melody. I can't tell you what to create. You have to create something that I have inspired within you. If I don't inspire anything inside of you, our connection will not be strong enough to open the portal. Not to mention, I will be a large failure as a muse."*

She knew he was trying to be funny to lighten the enormity of what he'd said. It didn't work. Melody's heart plummeted into her stomach. It was all up to her. The only way she would be able to bring Liron to her was through her love and her creation. She understood why he had been reluctant to tell her. He was afraid her love for him wasn't strong enough. Of course he would think that. He was hell-bent on believing that she was going to desert him too.

What disturbed her more than anything was the fact that she was afraid it wouldn't work either. Not because her love wasn't strong enough, but because she knew, in order to open the portal, she had to venture back to a place she really had no desire to go.

Which brought her back to the locked door.

Melody thought she had been doing good with playing the piano again. Now, she had to take a trip back into her past and try to reconnect with a part of her she had forced into being dormant. She'd never wanted to write music again. Not after what had happened. Why would she when all it did was remind her of what she had lost?

But now...

Now, it was different. Her parents had been taken from her by unforeseen circumstance. If she chose to keep the door locked because she was too afraid of the pain she would have to go through, she was making a deliberate, conscious choice to lose Liron. Because that's what would happen. She would lose him forever.

He had confronted his past, which was just as painful as hers in a different way, in order to find the key to enable them to be together again. If she refused to do the same because of her own cowardice, then she was no better than his ex-wife. She would have turned her back on him too.

And despite the sorrow of her parents being gone, the pain of dealing with those bottled up memories would be small in comparison to losing Liron for all time.

Drawing in a deep breath, she stepped forward, turned the key in the lock, and flung the door open.

She wasn't sure what she expected. Ghosts and skeletons and wispy things like in the horror movies? It was definitely not that dramatic. Real ghosts didn't exist. Only ones that the mind conjured up out of fear, doubt, and regret. In some ways, she imagined those were worse. She would have preferred the paranormal to the cold, dusty, cluttered room chock full of everything she had been trying to block out of her mind.

Maybe trying to avoid it for all this time had been a stupid idea. A person couldn't run from their issues. She knew that. Everyone said it. She had said it in the past also. It was different when the shoe was on the other foot. Easy to say, difficult to do.

Resigning herself to the fact that there was really no easy way to go about this, and that she was just going to have to barrel on in there, Melody went into the room and turned the light on. Her eyes scanned over her father's cello, propped up against the wall in its case, and her mother's violins—she had about four, two electric, one old, beat up antique-looking thing, and her regular one—laid out next to it. Over in the far corner were Melody's old viola, guitar, flute, and some other random things. A tambourine. A clarinet she had never learned to play. Some maracas.

All of her parents' clothes were hanging in the closet. She hadn't been able to get rid of them. Stacks of photo albums were piled around, along with boxes of her parents' possessions that had been too painful to keep in the main part of the house, but she couldn't bear to part with.

With a sigh, she allowed the memories to flow through her, agonizing as they were, and headed over to the far end of the room where a box full of her old sheet music was. She sat down cross-legged on the floor and began to sift through it, looking for the lost pages of the concerto she had been attempting to write.

She didn't know how long she was in there. She lost track of time. There was a memory attached to each piece of music, and after she'd gone through that, she'd moved on to pictures, clothing, things. She revisited what she had been avoiding for so long, laughed and cried, allowing her grief to work through her in its entirety and accepting the loss instead of pretending like it wasn't there.

By the time she had finished, she'd located the few poorly-written pages of her concerto and was beyond exhausted. She ate a meager dinner, vowed to start on her music the next morning, and practically fell into bed. She felt like she was on a runaway train of emotion that showed no signs of stopping. She was drained and worn out, and felt the enormity of the task she was about to undertake weighing on her shoulders.

She hadn't composed anything in so long. What if she couldn't do it? What if she failed? If she wasn't good enough, wasn't talented enough to create a masterpiece worthy of Liron, she would lose him. She couldn't bear the thought of losing him also. It would be too much. She would never recover.

The future she wanted so desperately and whether or not she was able to attain it was all up to her. That should have been comforting, but it wasn't. It was overwhelming. Far worse than having to pass chemistry in order to graduate high school. Far worse than her audition to get into Juilliard. Far worse than graduating Juilliard, and even worse still than her audition for a place in the orchestra.

This was a test beyond all tests. She was trying to bend the laws of the universe. How could she even hope to accomplish something like that? She was just one woman. Just an ordinary, human woman who played the piano and who, at one time, had dabbled at composition. She was no one special at all…

With her exhausted mind unable to continue freaking out, Melody slowly dropped into sleep, and right before she conked out into the deep sleep where dreams are not found, she heard Liron's voice like a whispering caress.

"You are special to me. Not only special, lovely. You are everything."

Chapter Eighteen

Two Weeks Later

The knocking on her door sounded distant, and she ignored it for a long while so that she could add the last few notes to the score she had been poring over like a madwoman. She stared at it when it was finished. Pages and pages of hand-written music—a symphony, a concerto, a masterpiece maybe. A score for her life. It was raw and painful. She had cried through most of it. She had never been more honest with herself.

It was her, and her parents, and Liron all in one.

Was it good enough? She didn't know. All she knew was that she had never put more of her own person into anything in her life.

The knocking continued to the point that she heaved a sigh, stood from where everything was strewn on her living room floor, and went to the door. If it was Rob, so help her, she was going to—

It wasn't Rob. It was Nikki, looking extremely concerned, and even more so now that Melody had opened the door.

She couldn't blame her. She must look horrendous. She'd been showering at least, but she'd been living in a tracksuit with her hair piled on top of her head in a haphazard knot for who knew how long.

Nikki raised an eyebrow. "Mel?" she questioned. "Are you okay?"

She sighed and stepped aside, opening the door to let her friend in. "I'm okay. I've just been...kinda busy."

Nikki frowned as she walked in and observed all the pages of music flung every which direction. "It looks like Beethoven blew up in here," she muttered. She knelt and picked up a page, examined it, and her eyes widened. She drew in a soft breath. "Mel...did you write this?"

Melody put her hands on her hips and shrugged.

Nikki stared at her with the oddest expression. "What made you decide to do this? I didn't even know when you got home from your rendezvous with Mr. Hottie on the coast. How long have you been doing this?"

"Two weeks." She ran her fingers through the loose strands of hair that had escaped her ponytail. "He helped me decide to do it, actually. It's just..." She heaved a sigh. "It's hard to explain. But I had to do it. I'm going to take it to the conductor of the orchestra I used to play in and see what he thinks." Over the last several conversations she'd had with Liron, it had come to her attention that creating something wasn't enough. That art had to be put into practice. It had to be displayed. She only hoped that her old conductor would think the score worthy.

"Geez...have you been doing anything else?" Nikki arched an eyebrow. "Eating? Sleeping?"

Melody laughed softly. "I've been eating when necessary, and sleeping." Sleep was the only time she got to speak with Liron, however minute those meetings were. She missed him so much she ached inside.

Nikki looked over some of the pages again, then sighed and looked up at Melody. She seemed to study her for a minute before asking, "Are you sure you're okay?"

Melody nodded. "I'm just kind of...spent. This was a little more grueling than I had anticipated."

"Why the rush?"

She couldn't exactly explain that to Nikki, so she shrugged. "Just felt like it had to get done, you know?"

Nikki smiled and caught Melody in a hug. "I'm proud of you, Mel. Really. You're finally finding yourself again. You're getting back in touch with your life and what you love."

No so much *what* she loved, but *who* she loved. She smiled. "Yeah, I guess you could say that."

The expression on her friend's face made Melody uneasy. Nikki almost looked as if she could sense something was a little askew. She frowned slightly. "How did things go with your boy-toy?" She opted for a lighthearted tone, but Melody knew Nikki better than that.

Her heart tumbled around in her chest like laundry in a

dryer. "Uh...it went well." She pushed back a few bedraggled pieces of hair.

Nikki cocked an eyebrow. "That's kind of vague."

"Well, he had some stuff he had to attend to, you know, and so did I. But he told me he would come to the performance if the Philharmonic approves my piece." The words rambled out of her mouth faster than anticipated.

To Nikki's credit, she didn't push the subject, but she didn't really look convinced either. "When are you going to take it to the conductor?"

"Tomorrow. After I go over it to make sure it's satisfactory." It had to be. She had practically poured her lifeblood into the thing. It couldn't be substandard. If she failed to find a way to have it played, thus failing to bring Liron back to her, she didn't know what she would do. She felt lost without him, so lonely it was suffocating.

Liron watched Siegfried as he hopped around on the sand, pecking at bugs and tormenting the seagulls. He had come down here every evening since Melody had left. He felt closest to her here, like she wasn't trapped a dimension away, alone and hurting. He knew she was hurting. He felt her distress even now. It was less intense than it had been. Instead of a violent storm of emotion, it was more of a dull, quiet, persistent ache. And exhaustion. He felt that from her above everything else.

The sunset had streaked the sky with crimson and gold, and the waves were calm and rhythmic. He sighed and glanced down at Siegfried as the bird hopped over, made a screeching noise, and peered up at him with intelligence in his golden eyes.

Liron smiled sadly. "I know, old friend. You haven't seen me this disheartened in a while. I'm sorry. I just miss her."

The bird tilted its head as if he had actually understood what Liron said, then screeched again and took to the skies for a sunset flight.

"He's beautiful."

Liron looked over his shoulder at the sound of the feminine voice and was surprised to see Samantha standing there. She was dressed much more subdued than before, in a calf-length, flowy black skirt and a red blouse that hugged her elegant frame. Regardless, she still looked every bit the aristocrat. Sophisticated and regal like royalty.

"Samantha, hello. What brings you out here?"

She sighed and came to sit next to him. The sunlight glinted off of her shining ebony hair and highlighted the delicate planes of her lovely face. He saw Elizabeth in her, all the dark beauty he had been so enamored with. Strange how that all seemed like it had happened to another person. He didn't feel the same any more.

"I haven't been to this area in a long while. I wasn't sure if I could remember where you lived." She smiled and looked up at him. "Then I remembered to look for the dark castle."

He chuckled. "Some things never change."

She gave a gentle laugh. "Thank goodness for that."

He frowned thoughtfully. "You came looking for me?"

She nodded and stretched her legs out in front of her. "When did you get a falcon?"

"A while ago." He studied her out of the corner of his eye, not trying to seem rude, but wondering why she was there at all. They were no longer connected in a way that she would feel obligated to him. "He has been a companion when I had few others. My parents live elsewhere now. I rarely see them. We correspond, but..." He shrugged.

Samantha gave him a wry smile. "Your parents never really did understand you, Liron. You were all music and beauty while they were all stoic logic and argument." She laughed again, a lovely musical sound. "I have no idea how a logic muse and a science muse birthed a music muse."

He chuckled. "Must have been way back in the lineage somewhere. I got that rogue gene from my great-great-great et cetera, et cetera grand-whatever."

"Were you able to find your wife?" she asked, sobering.

Liron heaved a sigh and looked down to study the patterns in the sand. "I am able to speak with her when she dreams. She is working on a way to get me to her, but I feel so helpless. I know she is exhausted, that the score she is writing to bring me to her world is taking everything out of her."

"It should make you feel loved to know she is going to such great lengths to be with you."

"It does, but I don't like knowing she is suffering and I am stuck here unable to do anything about it."

She smiled and reached over to cover his hand with hers. "Everything will work out in the end, Liron. Don't have such a dismal look on your face. You are too handsome to scowl so much." He cocked an eyebrow at her and she giggled. "You were always brilliant, but such a pessimist. Not that I blame you after everything that happened. Have some faith in your Melody. From what you told me, she must possess a rare kind of power to do what she did. I know you worry about her, but she is stronger than you give her credit for." A teasing sparkle came to life in her eyes. "As are most women." At his smile, she squeezed his hand and withdrew. "I was speaking to Raymond after you came to see me, and we've decided that once everything is said and done and back to normal, we would like you and your wife to come one night for dinner."

Liron couldn't pretend not to be shocked at the invitation. It had been so long since he had even associated with Samantha or anyone in her family. She was the sister of his ex-wife. It would have been an awkward situation any way a person looked at it.

Samantha seemed to sense his bewilderment and she smiled. "It's been so long since everything that happened with Elizabeth. She is gone in both this realm and the other. It is silly to hold onto the past in such a way that prevents us from being friends. I always thought you were such a brilliant and gentle man, and it makes me happy to know that you have finally found your perfect mate. If it doesn't make you uncomfortable, I would like it if we could be in one another's lives again. It has been far too long since Raymond and I had dinner guests. We desperately desire some good food, some laughter, and a little bit of music."

Liron found himself smiling at the invitation, and surprisingly, the idea didn't make him uncomfortable at all. He found this slightly strange considering, at any other time, it probably would have. He wouldn't have wanted to face the memories that being around Samantha would resurrect. Now, the memories that had been the cause of so much of his lonely sorrow over the years were only that—memories. Nothing more, nothing less. They no longer hurt. They just...were.

Melody had healed him in every single way.

A pang shot through his heart at the knowledge. He wanted to hold her, kiss her, make love to her all night long and then again in the morning until there was no space in her mind or her heart left to wonder how much he cherished her.

It disturbed him that that tiny spot of doubt still lingered within him. Way in the back, where he tried not to let his mind go, he heard the whispered, *What if this doesn't work? What if you don't mean as much to her as she does to you? What if you never inspired her at all and are unable to get to her? What if all of this was just a tormenting but temporary dream?*

Samantha's sigh brought him out of his wandering thoughts, and he looked up to see her regarding him with a chastising expression. He arched an eyebrow in question.

"It may have been a long time since I've seen you, Liron Tabor, but I know what a man looks like when he's feeling sorry for himself, and what a man looks like when he's doubting everything he shouldn't be doubting." She stood, brushed the sand off of her skirt, and held her hand out to him. "Come on."

He frowned. "Come on and what?" Even as he asked it, he slid his fingers in her hand and let her tug him up.

She slipped her arm through his and started to guide him back up the beach. "I'm taking you back to my house tonight so you can stop wallowing. Raymond's been dying for someone to play chess with, and that is not my game of choice."

"I'm terrible at chess," Liron muttered.

"Oh, don't worry. So is he. Feel free to cheat as much as you like."

The laughter that bubbled up from Liron's chest felt nice, and despite the less than ideal situation he currently found himself in, it was wonderful to feel like he had friends in his life again. He had been so isolated for so many years. There was a chance to have so much more with Melody.

Because of Melody.

All of the beauty he was experiencing in his life as of late was because of her.

And it would all crash into blackness if he could not be with her.

This plan had to work. There was no other option, and no other outcome he would settle for.

If she chewed on her fingernails anymore, she was pretty sure she wasn't going to have any left. She had never really been a gnaw-on-the-nails type of person, but this situation was different. If this blew up in her face, her whole world would come crashing down around her.

Two days ago, she'd gone to the music director—also the conductor—of the Philharmonic she had once been a part of. She'd shown him her score, which he had been insanely impressed with. He'd been optimistic about the possibility of it being performed at the fall concert that was being planned for two months from now, but Melody knew it would have to be run past the Board of Directors before any final decisions were made.

So, that was what she was currently awaiting. Their decision. It was like torture. How long did it take to deliberate on whether her music score was terrible or not?

After about forty-five minutes, the music director came out into the hall where she was waiting and beckoned her to go inside the small conference room.

A tingle of apprehension ran down Melody's spine as she stood and followed him inside. All of her parents' old friends and colleagues stared back at her as she entered, people she had once considered her friends as well. She had never imagined facing them could be so daunting.

The music director pulled a chair out for her at the foot of the table and she sat, grateful for that simple luxury as her knees were shaking so badly she was surprised no one could hear them knocking.

The music director resumed his seat at the head of the table and met Melody's gaze with a smile. He raised his hands and indicated everyone else present. "Melody, please stop looking like you're about to find out if you passed or failed the final exam. You are one of the finest musicians to come out of Juilliard in the last ten years, you are a remarkable pianist, and your parents were dear members of this orchestra, as well as all of our friends. Did you really think any of us would deny you?"

Melody fought back tears and averted her eyes to the table. She shook her head. "I don't want you to play my score because you feel like you owe my family or me something. I don't want your pity. I know it might not be that good. I've never composed anything before—"

The music director cut her off with a snort and a laugh. "Well, perhaps you should start." She looked up at him in bewilderment, and he folded his hands in front of him on the table. There was a twinkle in his hazel eyes when he smiled at her. "This score is wonderful, Melody. From the dreary, haunting first movement to the sweeping finale. Reading the music is one thing. I cannot wait to hear it performed. This decision was unanimous." He held up his index finger. "On one condition."

She arched an eyebrow.

"You must agree to be the guest conductor for the piece." She felt like someone had jolted her, and she started to protest, but he shushed her. "It is your music, Melody. It is only right that you lead the orchestra in playing it. Please, say you'll do it."

She stared, uncomprehending, for a few moments before she let out the air she had been holding in a slow breath of surrender. She nodded slowly.

The music director clapped his hands together with a grin. "Excellent. Rehearsals will begin two weeks from now. Although,"—he slid the music score across the table to Melody—"it needs a title."

Melody stared at the empty space at the top of the first page, at a loss. She hadn't even thought of what to call it.

"We all wondered what you were up to, holed away for all this time," an elderly woman at her right said suddenly. "Have you been working on this all year?"

Melody shook her head absently. "Just the last two weeks."

"Two weeks?" The woman's voice went up to a shrill pitch. "That is remarkable! What inspired you?"

Melody swallowed hard as her mind filled with a hundred rapid-fire memories. Her parents' deaths, the funeral, loneliness, so much aching loneliness, Liron's music, Liron himself, the beauty and wonder he had shown her. The passion for music he had rekindled within her. All she had ever known and all she had ever loved flashed through her at high speed and a small smile lifted her lips. "My life," she murmured. "The life I had, and the life I want."

And, just like that, she knew what her score needed to be called.

She picked up a pen and scrawled across the top of the page, *Liron's Melody.* Because the music was for him. It was about him. It was because of him.

And regardless of whatever may be, she was his.

Chapter Nineteen

Two months later

"Liron, seriously, stop fidgeting."

He couldn't. He'd never been more nervous in his entire life. He huffed out a breath and turned when Samantha's hand on his shoulders forced him away from the mirror. "Do I look completely idiotic?" he muttered.

Her easy smile gleamed and she shook her head, sending her teardrop earrings swinging. "You look stunning." She smoothed the lapels of his black suit jacket.

"I haven't felt this ridiculous since I married your sister." It was true in so many ways. While he was never slovenly in appearance, there was rarely a call for him to dress in formal attire, and doing so made him feel awkward. Not only that, but he had no idea if this was going to work, and if it didn't, he would be spending the greater part of the evening sitting in his living room, which wouldn't merit the suit and tie. Not to mention, if it *did* work, he'd suddenly find himself in the human realm, in a foreign location, looking for Melody amongst a bunch of foreign people. None of these options seemed to be a compelling reason for him to calm down.

"Liron, you married the girl already. The scary part is over."

Liron glanced over at Raymond, Samantha's husband, lounging on his bed like he owned the universe. In all his life, Liron had never met such a laid-back muse as Ray. But he was jovial, and fun, and caring, and he looked at Samantha like she walked on water. He had grown somewhat fond of the man over the course of the last two months.

In all reality, Liron had to be grateful for the small things. Even though it had come about by a set of circumstances he would have preferred to avoid, Melody being stuck in her world had given him a reason to visit Samantha, something he never would have done without prompting. Because of this, he had been able to rekindle a friendship he'd thought long past its expiration date.

And if he was going to be honest with himself, he had no idea how he would have gotten through the past two months without Samantha and Ray's friendship. They had stepped up to alleviate the crushing weight of emptiness that Melody's absence had left, had kept him occupied and laughing, and had helped him remain sane.

Liron glanced down at Samantha, who continued to fuss over him, adjusting his clothing and whatnot. He then glanced over at Ray who, being a lyrical muse, was submersed in a book of poetry. Seeing this, and knowing that he would be granted a small moment of privacy, he grasped onto Samantha's hand and gave a little tug.

She looked up at him in question.

He knew he looked pained. He had to. Because he *felt* pained. "Sam...what if this doesn't work?"

Sympathy reflected in her eyes, and she pulled him over to stand in front of his stained glass bedroom window so that they had a semblance of their own space. "Liron, stop fretting. Of course it will work. She felt enough of your soul to become so captivated with your music that she came across the barrier between our worlds. That has never happened, at least not to my knowledge. You think she has that kind of power, but does not possess the talent to bring you into her world? Something that is readily more heard of than the former?"

He shook his head. "It's not her talent that I doubt."

"Only her love." Samantha fixed him with a chastising expression.

He couldn't even argue with her. It wasn't so much her love he doubted. It was just....

Samantha sighed and reached down to take his hands in hers. "Liron, I know my sister did a number on you, and because of that I know some part of you is always waiting for the other shoe to drop. You believe that Melody is too good to be true, that sooner or later, it's all going to end and you're going to be alone and heartbroken again."

He averted his eyes, his heart aching dully in his chest at that possibility, and at the truth of her words.

She shook her head and gave him a small smile. "You'll never get anywhere dwelling on things that have long since been and gone. Elizabeth did what she did *ages ago.* Melody is not her. Melody loves you. This *will* work."

Her conviction bolstered him, and he sucked in his breath, squaring his shoulders in some kind of gesture of mock courage. He met Samantha's eyes. "If it does work...." At her stern expression, he cleared his throat. "*When* this works, I'm going to need something to eventually bring me back home. So, if you could do me a favor, and say, a couple hours or so after I go through the portal, you and Ray do something to bring me back. Scream, yell, dance a jig. I don't know. Just, something that will get my attention. Considering the way it used to work with Melody, and providing it works the same on that end of things, the fact that you are in my home and causing a ruckus should be enough to trigger the portal."

She nodded. "All right. A couple hours, you say?"

"Somewhere around there. That should be more than enough time in the human world to get everything settled."

"Consider it done, Liron."

His heart softened, and he filled with warmth and affection for the woman in front of him. "Sam...." He sighed and shook his head, at a loss for any adequate words. "Thank you so much for everything over these last couple months. I..."

She shushed him softly and gave him a warm smile. "Liron, you were my family once. I would like to think you still are. I only wish I'd stopped being such a coward sooner."

He smiled. "I was just as much of a coward. None of that matters now. I'm grateful to have you and Ray in my life."

A playful expression lit up her face. "And hopefully your Melody is better at chess than you. I didn't think anyone could be worse than Ray 'til you came along."

Liron chuckled and felt momentarily better about everything that was about to occur. Samantha had a way of taking all the dreariness out of a situation, and he was grateful for that.

He had done everything he could on his end.

Now, all he had to do was wait.

And hope.

Melody wasn't quite sure what she was feeling as she stood in the wings backstage, waiting for the concert to begin. The orchestra was playing one piece—a Rachmaninoff—then they would perform hers before the twenty minute intermission.

She wasn't nervous about the piece. Not really. She had rehearsed so many times with everyone that she could conduct it inside, outside, backwards, on her head, and in her sleep. That wasn't an issue.

She was so terrified that what she'd created would fall short, that her music would fail to bring Liron to her. Everyone kept telling her how wonderful it was, but she had a hard time comprehending that she could create something remarkable enough to do Liron justice. And she knew that if she failed, the last remaining piece of her heart would shatter into irrevocable damage.

The last two months had been lonely without Liron, but she'd had a lot to keep her busy. Rehearsals and loose ends that needed to be tied up should everything go according to plan. Plus, she was at least able to speak with him in her dreams, which was better than nothing, regardless of how fleeting it was.

The orchestra was tuning up on stage as the audience filed in, and the hum of it filled her with memories of long ago. Somehow, they weren't as horrendous as they had once been. She had been forced to confront so much of her past during this process.

So much of what she had been running from she'd had to meet head-on in order to get tasks accomplished integral to the running smoothly of the concert. It had been painful, but also strangely therapeutic. While she still felt the hole in her heart that her parents had once inhabited, it wasn't as all-consuming as it had once been. Now, it was only a dull ache. Present, but not overwhelming. And it no longer centered itself around music. Fear of playing, of embracing what her parents had loved so much, had finally faded.

Suddenly, the lights in the house of the theatre dimmed and a hush fell over the audience. Melody's stomach dipped and plummeted. There were so many things swirling around in her mind at once.

She didn't want to mess up. That was a big one. Typical holy-cow-I'm-in-the-spotlight jitters. And she was afraid no one was going to like her music. While she knew not everyone had the same taste, she hoped the audience at least appreciated what it was and didn't think it sounded like a sixth grader had been let loose in a music room and had decided to mesh all the instruments together in a terrible, jumbled mess.

All of the orchestra members assured her it didn't sound like that, even the ones who had joined after the accident, hadn't known her parents, and therefore, didn't have to feel guilty if they told her how much it sucked. She supposed that should count for something, but she still felt apprehensive about unveiling her music to a theatre full of people. It was her life put to notes. It was personal. But, then again, she imagined all art was.

She wondered what her parents would think if they were alive. What would they think of her concerto? Of Liron? She smiled to herself. What was she thinking? They would have adored Liron, would probably have ended up going to live in his world also.

She could just imagine her happy-go-lucky father and her beautiful, eccentric mother in the marketplace letting loose with the other muses. Her mother would probably want one of the rebel muses to teach her how to fire dance.

She could see it all so clearly in her mind, and she wished with all her heart that they could be there to experience the magnificent world she had stumbled upon. Where creativity was embraced and cherished, where emotions weren't taboo, and where gorgeous men produced sinfully erotic music when they touched you.

Her heart skipped a beat at the thought of Liron. This was her one chance—her only chance. If she messed this up, if she wasn't good enough, she would never see him again, never touch him again. He would only exist in her dreams like some kind of insane person's fantasy. So much was riding on this one moment....

She shook her head. She couldn't think like that. She had to believe this would work, that all of this hadn't been for nothing. She had to believe that when her twenty minutes of fame were over, Liron would be with her again, and they could begin their life together amidst art and music and splendor.

"Melody?"

She tore herself out of her thoughts and glanced up at the stage manager in front of her.

"You're on after this announcement."

It was only then that Melody heard the thunderous applause signaling the end of the first piece. Her heart kicked into double-time when she heard the music director's voice echoing through the theatre.

"A year ago, this orchestra lost three members who were very dear to all of us. Eric and Anna Hoffman, our lead cellist and violinist, were killed in a tragic car accident, and their daughter, Melody Hoffman, our pianist, resigned her position with the Philharmonic shortly after. It is with great pleasure tonight that we welcome back Ms. Hoffman, but no longer as our pianist. Tonight, she takes the stage as our guest conductor to lead us in her own composition, a concerto entitled, *Liron's Melody.* So, without further ado, please welcome Ms. Melody Hoffman."

The applause spurred her into action, and Melody sucked in a deep breath before striding out onto the stage. She shook the music director's hand with a smile, then took the baton he offered and went to her place up in front of the orchestra.

She swallowed hard, closed her eyes, and took a deep, calming breath. *This is just like rehearsal*, she told herself as she raised her hands to the ready position. She told herself not to pay attention to all the eyes staring at her, both in front and behind. *This is it. Your one shot. You can do this, Mel. For Liron. For your parents. For yourself. It's now or never.*

She sucked in her breath and counted a four-count before the orchestra launched into the first movement of her piece.

There were three movements that made up Melody's composition, depicting three distinct stages of her life. The first movement was entitled, "Tragedy," for obvious reasons. It was mournful and haunting, dreary in its musical rendition of the year Melody had spent aching for a life she would never again know.

The second movement was entitled, "Awakening," again, for obvious reasons. This one also began with a gothic flair, but gradually grew into a melodious dedication to Liron and the beauty he had brought back to her life. It included lively Celtic elements, an ode to the wonderful night they'd spent in the marketplace, and the end left the audience with a feeling of hope and joy.

The third movement was entitled, "Future," and was the most complex of the three. It featured every section of the orchestra at some point and combined them all into a sweeping, atmospheric finale that represented the future Melody wanted to have with Liron. She had tried her best to incorporate instruments that would reflect the sounds of nature—thunder, the ocean, wind in the trees, as well as all the classical complexities of man-made instruments. It sounded like an epic love song, which she imagined it was, and it ended with passion and conviction.

She lost herself in the music, reliving every part of her life that had inspired it. It was different playing it for an audience than it was in rehearsal. Everything felt rawer, truer somehow.

She felt Liron within the notes, just as she had felt her parents, and just as she felt herself. He was with her. She knew this. He was with her because he had become a part of her. He had given her back her love of music. He had brought her back to life. His flame would burn within her for all time.

When the music came to an end, Melody's heart pounded both from exertion and emotion. The tremendous applause from the audience let her know that at least they hadn't hated it, and a lump of overwhelming emotion clogged her throat when each member of the orchestra started to stand, one by one, and applaud as well.

Tears burned behind her eyes and she gave the musicians a smile and a nod of appreciation and thanks. Slowly, she turned around to face the audience, expecting a miracle.

But all she saw was a sea of strangers. No familiar face stood out among them. She glanced up to the balcony, but it was impossible to see anything up there but shadow. Her heart dropped so low she didn't know if it was still in her body. An aching, gaping hole opened up where her heart had once been and the emotional tears she had been fighting a moment ago turned to tears of profound despair.

If the music had worked, if the portal had been opened, Liron would be somewhere in her line of sight. It had opened for her right in his living room. But he was nowhere. He was gone.

She had failed.

Melody went through the motions of bowing to the audience and going through the required polite formalities, but once she stepped off the stage and the lights in the house went up for intermission, something worse than the wave of heartbreak she had felt swarmed her. Emptiness. Numbness. Her tears evaporated and she suddenly felt nothing but dismal cold.

She walked back to the dressing room she had been given and closed the door behind her, requiring privacy. She sat down in front of the mirror and stared at her reflection. She'd opted to wear the traditional black of a classical concert and was in a long, elegant dress that hugged her body in all the right places. It had a low back and a deep sweetheart neckline. It was sexy enough to turn some heads, but classy enough for the event. At her neck, she'd decided to wear a garnet necklace since she'd left the one her mother had given her back in Liron's home. She'd left her blonde hair down in gentle waves. She'd done smoky eye makeup with a soft blush, and had felt beautiful upon leaving the house.

But it had all been for nothing. Her music had not brought Liron to her, and her heart would never beat normally again. It would never hear his rapturous song, and she would never feel his music surging through her veins.

Heaviness unlike anything she had ever felt pressed on her chest and her shoulders sagged in defeat. She suddenly felt so very tired.

A knock on the door made her jump, and she looked up to see the stage manager stick her head in. "Melody, you have someone here to see you."

Her heart tripped over itself trying to change from its sluggish beat to beating way too fast. "Send him in," she said breathlessly.

Before the stage manager could even get out of the way, Nikki came bulldozing through the door.

Melody's heart fell back down into that hollow place. "Nikki," she said. She forced a smile, hoping it would hide the flat tone her voice had to it.

"Oh my goodness, Melody! That music was wonderful! I

would have waited until after the show to tell you, but I just couldn't. I had to come and see you. That was so amazing!"

Nikki was dressed in a sunny yellow dress with her dark hair pulled back. She looked stunning, and Melody gave a small, sad smile, happy at least to have her friend with her. "Thanks," she murmured.

Nikki frowned. "Is he here?"

Melody swallowed hard and looked up at her friend. She shook her head, feeling tears threaten again.

Nikki knelt down in front of Melody and took her hands. "He will be."

The heavy feeling on Melody's chest started to become constricting and crushing. "I don't think so, Nikki..."

She sighed. "Look, Mel. I'm not even going to pretend that I don't know something strange is going on. I can't place my finger on it anyway. It's just a feeling I get. But I know whatever is going on between you and Liron is not conventional, is it?"

Melody glanced into her friend's brown eyes and shook her head.

Nikki squeezed Melody's hands. "I have no idea what that means. Part of me thinks maybe I don't even want to know...do I want to know?"

"Probably not," Melody said with a watery giggle.

She smiled. "Okay, I'm going to take your word on that. But that same instinct telling me there is something completely bizarre about this entire situation is also telling me that you shouldn't give up. He'll be here, Melody. I know it."

One tear succeeded in escaping, and it ran a track down Melody's cheek. "No, he won't, Nik. I blew it. He was depending on me and I blew it."

She frowned. "Blew it how?"

Just then, the stage manager came back in again. "The intermission is over in five more minutes, Melody," she said. "The music director, as well as the entire orchestra, has asked me to tell you that they would like you to play an encore after the last piece. That is, if you happen to have something prepared."

Melody stared at the woman for a long moment. "They want me to *play?*"

The stage manager nodded with a smile. "I don't think

you really understand how much you and your family were loved here."

Melody let out a long, loud exhale and tossed the idea around for a minute. Her first instinct was to decline. The pressure was too much and it was too short of notice. She had no idea what she would even perform.

But as she mulled on it, she knew exactly what she would play. And she knew she had to do it. She had nothing left to lose, and regardless of the fact that she had failed Liron, she couldn't continue to dwell in the past. She had to say good-bye to the life she had once known. It was the only way she could move forward. She had learned that through all of this, if nothing else.

She glanced at Nikki, then back up to the stage manager. "All right, I'll do it. I have something I can play."

Chapter Twenty

The silence of the theatre was deafening as she sat at the piano that had been set up on the stage for her encore. Her fingers were poised over the keys, and everyone was waiting. It felt like time was moving through cold honey. Her breathing sounded insanely loud and her heartbeat drowned out everything else.

The music director had announced her after the last piece of music, saying, "Please welcome Ms. Hoffman back to the stage for one final performance."

She'd smiled, walked tall out to the piano, and took her seat. No one would know that inside her, one world was ending and another one was fading, leaving her with empty space and nothingness. A blank slate. She had no idea where she was going to go from here.

But it didn't matter right now. She would have to deal with the specifics soon enough. Now, all that she needed to do was play this piece of music. She needed to heal from the losses of the past and grieve for the loss in her present. To do any of that she needed to play.

This piece.

Play.

She drew in a deep breath and her fingers descended onto the keys, playing the notes she knew so well and had shied away from for so long. The beginning measures of "Adagio in G Minor" began to fill the theatre. As she played, memories of her parents flooded her mind, but strangely, none of them were of their funeral, which is what she had equated the song with ever since then.

They were of her childhood and all the laughter and love she had experienced with them, all the musical adventures. Memories of every concert she had ever played in middle school, high school, at Juilliard, and how her mom and dad were always in the first row cheering the loudest. She remembered every Saturday music session, every rehearsal for the Philharmonic, every opera and ballet and music concert they had gone to see together. She remembered the beauty and the light her parents had brought into her life instead of the sorrow and blackness that had come with their departure.

She lost herself in the notes of the music, gave herself over to it completely. She played like it was the last piece of music she would ever perform. And she whispered a silent goodbye in her heart, a final farewell to her parents who were gone, but would never be forgotten. It wasn't them she was saying goodbye to. It was the grief that had been her constant companion ever since the accident. She didn't need it anymore. She could finally let it go.

Because of one man. Because of what he had shown her in the brief time he had touched her life. Because of the love of music he had resurrected inside of her.

Maybe she was never meant to keep him. Maybe he had only been allowed in her life long enough to show her how to live, to breathe again. Maybe he was only meant to be her muse and nothing more.

Whatever reason Liron had been in her life, he had changed it for the better. He had helped her remember how to live and not merely exist. He had helped her heal. She would never turn her back on that gift.

Melody pounded out the last part of the song, surrendering completely to the music, letting it flow through her like her tumultuous emotions, and letting the tragic notes soothe her as her heart bled.

The last note echoed through the room, followed by several seconds of utter silence. She noticed vaguely that tears were streaming down her cheeks, but paid them little attention as the audience and the orchestra members behind her burst into uproarious sound.

She lifted her head and glanced out at the audience. Everyone was on their feet clapping wildly and cheering in a way that would be much more fitting at a sporting event. A small, genuinely joyous laugh bubbled through her chest and she stood, giving several deep bows. Then, she turned to the orchestra, who were yelling and applauding in the same fashion, and bowed to them as well.

The music director appeared from the wings of the stage carrying an enormous bouquet of red roses and more tears filled her eyes—these of appreciation and genuine wonder at the kindness of her former orchestra members.

She took the roses and cradled them in her arms while the director pressed a kiss to her cheek. She turned and bowed for the audience one more time, then swept her arm wide to indicate the orchestra behind her. The audience continued to cheer loudly, and the rest of the musicians gave a unanimous bow.

Since it was the end of the concert, the musicians started to file off the stage in a precision-like manner. Melody took her leave as well, but started toward the other side of the stage to avoid the stampede of the orchestra members.

The lights in the house came up so that the audience could see where they were going, and Melody glanced out at them as she started toward the wings. She scanned the packed theatre and smiled to herself, then stopped dead in her tracks as her eyes were drawn to a solitary figure standing along the far back wall.

She frowned and her heart did a strange *ker-thump.* She peered closer at the stoic form, still having difficulty seeing clearly due to the low light and the shadows the balcony cast down onto the main floor. He stood tall and lean, with broad shoulders and hair that flowed to those shoulders.

A rush of cold heat passed through her and she felt the color drain from her face. She stumbled to the edge of the stage and looked out, knowing she must appear slightly crazed, but not caring.

Slowly, the figure she was desperately trying to get a good look at stepped forward into better light.

The cold wave of heat that had pooled around her stomach exploded into fiery tingles along every surface of her body, and she tripped herself on her high heels and practically broke her ankle wheeling around and scrambling off the stage's side steps.

She dashed through the dispersing crowd, darting around people like she was in some kind of pinball machine, and came to a screeching halt in front of the most glorious sight she had ever beheld. She couldn't speak, couldn't even move. All she could do was stare at his beautiful face, at his blue eyes that were sparkling with joy and his wonderful smile that lit up every corner of her heart that had withered only moments before.

He was dressed in a black suit with a deep burgundy-colored shirt and a black silk tie. He looked so striking it was ridiculous. Tears filled her eyes and hovered there while her heart did tumbling motions that robbed her of breath. "Are you a hallucination?" she rasped.

He gave her a lopsided grin, gently took the roses from her, and set them down, then slipped an arm around her waist and pulled her close against his chest. "What kind of a hallucination would I be if I told you?" he whispered against her ear.

Melody's eyelids fluttered closed as sensual, smoldering notes drifted leisurely through her mind, igniting similar sensual, smoldering fire in her body. Her breath rushed out of her in heady relief, and her tears finally succeeded in falling. She buried her face against his neck, breathing in his scent, lavishing in it, and snuggling so close to him she may as well have been attached. "I thought I'd failed," she muttered against the collar of his shirt.

"What?" He took her gently by the shoulders and pulled back just enough to see her. He wiped the tears from her cheeks with tender fingers.

"After my concerto...you weren't here. I-I thought I'd failed, that I wasn't good enough, that what I'd created wasn't good enough." More tears descended under the onslaught of her emotional rollercoaster ride.

He frowned. "Weren't good enough? Are you insane? I never want to hear you say those words again. If I had not been able to come here tonight, it would have been failing on my part, not on yours. It would have meant that I hadn't inspired you enough."

"Liron, I don't care whose failing it would have been. It doesn't matter. *Where were you?* I thought my whole life was over." She let out a little sob, feeling like a neurotic spaz.

Liron gave a soft chuckle and pulled her back into his arms, holding her close and burying his fingers in her hair. "Well, unfortunately, I had no control over where the portal decided to open. So I ended up in the janitor's closet. Took me a bit to find my way out. When I finally did, they wouldn't let me into the theatre because I didn't have a ticket. I loitered around in the lobby until intermission, when I snuck in and hid in the dark back here like some kind of criminal."

She laughed in spite of herself, her turbulent emotions subsiding. She wrapped her arms around Liron's waist and held on, relishing in the solidness, the *realness*, of him. "I thought I'd lost you," she said on a sigh.

His arms tightened around her. "Never. I would have found a way. I can't let you go. I won't."

She pulled back and looked up at him. "You don't have to." She grasped him behind the neck and pulled his head down to crush his lips to hers. He responded immediately, bringing his hands up to cradle her face while he deepened the kiss and possessed her completely with his mouth and his music as it invaded her mind, heart, and body. Every lonely space, every cold recess within her that had appeared at being unable to return to him, incinerated. The pieces of her annihilated heart fused back together under the velvet assault of his lips, and the dank despair she suffered while in the human world disappeared. If she'd had any doubt in her mind about returning to his world with him, that would have been enough to decide her.

Her link to her world had died with her parents. Now, she knew she belonged amongst the muses.

"You taste sweeter than I remember," he whispered over her lips. "Like a spice I will never get enough of."

She grinned and snuggled close to him, reveling in his warmth and his unyielding strength. During all the worst turmoil of her emotional journey, Liron had been her strength. And when he'd needed her the most, she had been his as well. She had never felt more fulfilled, more satisfied.

"Are we going to be able to go back home now?" she questioned.

He nodded. "I have asked Samantha and Raymond to cause some kind of hoopla in order to get my attention and trigger the portal. They are waiting for us back at my house."

Melody gave Liron a flat expression, trying to ignore the spasm of jealousy that rippled through her at the mention of the other woman. "Seems like you and Samantha have become rather close over the last two months," she grumbled.

His lips twitched in amusement. "Yes, I imagine we have.

I am pretty sure she has an ulterior motive, though."

Her eyes snapped up to his, and she scowled fiercely. "Like what?"

Liron trailed his fingers through her hair and sighed in an exaggerated fashion. "Well, I'm pretty sure she's only hanging around with me because she so desperately wants to meet this legendary wife of mine who can defy the laws of physics and bend the universe to her will."

Melody felt heat color her cheeks at both the praise and at her ridiculous, possessive assumption. "Oh." She smiled bashfully. "Well, I guess I can live with that."

He laughed and nuzzled her nose with his. "You have nothing to be worried about, lovely." He whispered the words over her lips in a tickling tease before claiming them again in another breathtaking kiss.

When Melody pulled away this time, she looked up at him with so much love in her heart she felt she would burst. She ran her palms up his chest and he made a happy noise in his throat and closed his eyes. She grinned and reached down to take his hand while she picked her roses up with the other one. "Come on. Let's go. I have a couple things I need to get from my house before we go. Just one suitcase."

He frowned and followed behind her toward backstage. "Only one?"

She nodded, and was stopped by the music director as they walked back up onto the stage.

"Melody!" he cried, enveloping her in an enthusiastic hug. "You were wonderful tonight! The way you played! And 'Adagio in G' of all things!"

She smiled softly. "Thank you. It was a wonderful experience." Liron's fingers tightened over hers, and her heart responded to his touch by skipping.

"Melody," he said, sobering. "I know this past year has been difficult for you, but we would love to have you back. Would you consider taking a place in the Philharmonic once again?"

She filled with warmth at the invitation and gave a soft sigh. "Thank you so much for the offer," she said, "but I'm actually moving."

He looked surprised. "Oh, really?"

She nodded. "Yes...out of the country, in fact. I need a

new start, you know?"

His eyes softened and he nodded in acceptance. "I understand. Thank you, Melody." He hugged her again. "For everything."

"No," she said, returning his embrace. "Thank you. You have done more than you even know."

He pulled back with a smile. "Just know that the invitation is always there for you."

"Thank you." She watched him walk away and glanced up at Liron to see him gazing at her with a gentle smile playing around his sensual lips. He didn't need to speak. All the love and pride he felt for her was reflected in his eyes. She raised herself up to press a tender kiss to his lips before continuing backstage.

"Mel!" Nikki cried when she entered the dressing room. "That song you played was—oh!" She stopped short and blinked up at Liron in surprise before a wide grin blossomed across her face. She glanced at Melody. "Is this him?"

Melody smiled. "Yes, Nikki, this is Liron. Liron, my friend Nikki."

Liron stepped forward, took Nikki's hand, and kissed the back of it. "A pleasure," he murmured.

Nikki stared at him with a bewildered and slightly adoring expression on her face before she shook her head and got a hold of herself. "L-Likewise," she stammered. She looked back at Melody. "I told you he would come."

Melody grinned, elation burbling inside of her like magma. Liron slid his arm around her shoulders and held her against his side. She fit comfortably there. A little frown creased her brow, and her smile faded as she realized that this would probably be the last time she would see her friend. A small bit of sadness crept in, and she swallowed hard. There was no way Nikki would be able to understand. She hated that she was going to hurt her. "Nik...I have something for you. It's at my house. Will you come by tomorrow? I'm going to leave the key in the flowerpot by the front door. Just let yourself in. Your gift is sitting on the piano...all right?"

Nikki's smile vanished like someone had waved a magic wand and that strange, knowing look came to life in her eyes again. Her gaze darted from Melody to Liron and back again. "Why can't you just give it to me?"

Melody chewed on her bottom lip, and she gained a small amount of comfort from the way Liron squeezed her shoulder. "I...I'm not going to be there, Nik."

Nikki stared at her for a long moment, as if tossing things around in her head, before her eyes grew glassy. "I'm not going to see you for a while, am I?" she rasped.

Melody's own eyes filled with tears—for the millionth time—and she shook her head as her throat constricted.

Nikki bit her bottom lip. "You're going somewhere, aren't you? Somewhere that I probably don't even want to know about because it's going to warp my brain in about five different ways, right?"

Melody laughed despite the sadness of the situation. "Yeah, probably."

The lip Nikki had been chewing on trembled and she darted her gaze to Liron again with a kind of pained expression. "Is he gonna kill you?" she blurted.

Melody startled. "What? Kill me? What in the world?"

Nikki took a daring step forward. "You know, go all bloodsucker on you and then turn you into some insanely beautiful...thing...you know...like *him*?"

Melody blinked at her friend for a few seconds. "Nikki, are you seriously asking me if Liron is a vampire?"

Nikki's face contorted, and she waved her hand at Liron. "Well...*look at him*! And all you tell me is that you're going somewhere and I'm not going to see you for a while! And I've had these weird heebie-jeebies ever since I came over after you'd finished your music score. I *knew* something abnormal was going on!"

Liron cleared his throat discreetly. "I assure you, I am not a vampire."

She stabbed her finger at him. "But you're...*something*, aren't you?" She looked over at Melody for the answer.

Melody sighed and nodded slowly.

The tears returned to Nikki's eyes. "Am I ever going to see you again?"

Melody stepped forward and caught her friend in an embrace. "I will try to come back and visit, Nik. I'm not sure when. I have to figure some stuff out first, okay? But I'll try." Nikki squeezed her hard and Melody's eyes stung.

"Are you happy, Mel?" she murmured.

Melody pulled away, met Nikki's eyes, and nodded vigorously at the knowledge that she was going back home, her real home...finally. "Yeah...I really am. I promise."

Warmth and affection filled Nikki's eyes even through her tears. "I'm glad then. You deserve it. Just promise me you'll keep playing."

Melody giggled, considering where she was headed. "I promise, Nik. I won't ever stop again." She hugged her one more time. "Remember to go to my house tomorrow."

Nikki nodded. "Goodbye, Mel."

"Goodbye." She pulled away and went back to Liron. She took his hand again and turned him back toward the exit. She wanted to get out of there. She didn't know how much time was left before Liron's friends called them back, and she didn't want the portal to the muse realm appearing out of nowhere and scaring the crap out of a bunch of unsuspecting people.

"One more thing!" Nikki called.

They both turned back to see her posturing at Liron in an almost threatening manner. She strode up to him with purpose and jabbed her finger into his chest. "Do you love her?"

Liron smiled softly, and his eyes filled with dark promises and voracious ardor as he looked down over at Melody. It was enough to set her blood ablaze and make her breath catch.

He looked back at Nikki. "I love her more than every song ever written, every note ever discovered, and every chord ever played in this world or any other."

Nikki's eyebrows shot up as her fierce expression turned to surprise. She blinked at him before letting her breath out in a *whoosh*. "Dang..." She looked at Melody. "Can I have one of these?"

Liron sidled up to Nikki with a demonic grin. "I'll send you someone," he murmured close to her ear. "He'll come in your dreams. Keep an eye out."

The color drained from Nikki's face, and she stared after them in stunned silence as Liron, looking entirely too pleased with himself, led them out the dressing room door.

Melody giggled. "Were you serious about sending a muse to Nikki?"

He shrugged one shoulder in a lazy movement. "I know a few people who might be interested. What does she do?"

"She's a teacher."

"Hmm…maybe a logic muse?"

Melody snorted and shook her head. "No way. Send her a rebel muse."

Liron cocked an eyebrow. "Oh, really?"

"Yeah. A big, hairy biker or something." Liron's laughter filled her with joy. He slipped his arm back around her shoulders as they headed out of the theatre.

"What did you leave her?" he asked.

She sighed. "Everything. The house. All of my things. I'm only taking one suitcase full of some clothing and some keepsakes, a few pictures of my family."

"Are you sure that's all you want?"

She looked up at him and smiled. "Yeah. I have what I need. Everything else is just stuff." She had been afraid to let go of all of her parents' things before because she'd been afraid that doing so would be like getting rid of them. But she knew now that wasn't the case. The love she had for her parents and the memories of them lived inside of her. They weren't attached to inanimate objects, and she didn't need things to bring them back to life, so to speak. They lived inside of her and always would. That was all she needed.

They took a cab back to Melody's house, where she finalized everything and made sure all was in order for Nikki tomorrow. She sighed, took one last look around at everything, at the life she was leaving behind, and bade a silent goodbye to it. One door had to close so she could open this new one that led to such spectacular things.

As if on cue, as soon as Melody had finished dragging her suitcase into the living room, a loud wheezing whine sound blasted through the room followed by a song that sounded like it had come straight out of Scotland. It was enough to cause both she and Liron to jump, and as soon as they'd recovered, they saw that half of Melody's living room had, once again, been transformed into Liron's.

Only, where there had once only been a dark room made of stone with a fireplace and a piano, there was now a man playing the bagpipes and a woman dancing around banging on a drum. Melody arched an eyebrow and looked up at Liron. "Your friends?" she assumed.

Liron blinked in bewilderment for a moment before a

rumbling laugh rolled out of him. "I had no idea he played the bagpipes."

There was a new kind of light in Liron's eyes, a happiness that had erased the shadowed, haunted look they had had before. It seemed that they had both found peace within themselves, and they had both made peace with their pasts. Now, all that lay before them was a bright and promising future full of new friends and wondrous music.

Liron bent down and grabbed Melody's suitcase, hurled it through the portal, then turned and faced her. He looked down at her, his blue eyes reflecting every beautiful thing she had ever seen, and he held his hand out to her.

She slowly eased her fingers into his and, as she did, magnificent, hauntingly rapturous notes danced throughout her entire body and wrapped around her heart, where she knew they would live, because that was where he lived. His song had become hers.

"You ready, lovely?" he murmured.

Her fingers tightened over his, and she reached her free hand up to run along his jaw. "Take me home, Liron."

He bent, lifted her into his arms, and kissed her thoroughly before carrying her, much like a newlywed in a romance movie—the kind with the grand, sweeping score—over the threshold to their future.

About the Author

Brieanna Robertson

    If someone were to ask me what I am, it could be summed up in one, simple word: Dreamer. Ever since I was a small child my imagination has run wild. I have been telling stories for as long as I can remember, creating grand worlds in my head and going on adventures that were invisible to others around me. Am I eccentric? Yes. Am I proud of that? Absolutely.

    I write about the things that inspire me, both in this world and in realms only seen with the imagination. My heroines are sassy and strong. My heroes are sometimes shy. I have an obsession with music (and musicians) and a fascination with wings. I believe true love does exist, and sometimes it is found in the strangest, most unexpected places. I also believe that family and close friends are the glue that hold people together.

Above all things, I believe in being true to yourself and seizing the day. Life is an amazing gift. Make your experience as beautiful as you possibly can.